BINNY IN SECRET

Binny
IN SECRET

HILARY McKAY
with illustrations by
MICAH PLAYER

Margaret K. McElderry Books
New York * London * Toronto * Sydney * New Delhi

MARGARET K. McELDERRY BOOKS
An imprint of Simon & Schuster Children's Publishing Division
1230 Avenue of the Americas, New York, New York 10020

Published by arrangement with Hodder Children's Books,
a division of Hachette Children's Books
First published in Great Britain in 2015 by Hodder Children's Books
First U.S. edition, 2015

MARGARET K. McELDERRY BOOKS is a trademark of Simon & Schuster, Inc.
For information about special discounts for bulk purchases, please contact Simon & Schuster Special Sales at 1-866-506-1949 or business@simonandschuster.com.
The Simon & Schuster Speakers Bureau can bring authors to your live event. For more information or to book an event, contact the Simon & Schuster Speakers Bureau at 1-866-248-3049 or visit our website at www.simonspeakers.com.
The text for this book is set in Bembo Std.
The illustrations for this book are rendered in ink and watercolor.
Manufactured in the United States of America
0516 OFF
First Margaret K. McElderry Books paperback edition June 2016
2 4 6 8 10 9 7 5 3 1
The Library of Congress has cataloged the hardcover edition as follows:
McKay, Hilary.
Binny in secret / Hilary McKay ; with illustrations by Micah Player. — First U.S. edition.
pages   cm
"First published in Great Britain in 2015 by Hodder Children's Books"—Copyright page.
Sequel to: Binny for short.
Summary: While getting bullied at school, twelve-year-old Binny investigates the disappearance of her brother's chicken and tries to save an endangered lynx.
ISBN 978-1-4424-8278-4 (hc) ★ ISBN 978-1-4424-8279-1 (pbk)
ISBN 978-1-4424-8280-7 (eBook)
[1. Family life—Fiction. 2. Schools—Fiction. 3. Bullying—Fiction. 4. Lynx—Fiction.]
I. Player, Micah, illustrator. II. Title.
PZ7.M4786574Bj 2015
[Fic]—dc23 ★ 2014033545

For my very special reader
Phoebe Maria Kitchener,
with lots of love from
Hilary McKay

List of Illustrations

BINNY IN SECRET

Chapter One

September the first, and the sort of burglar wind that plucked litter from trash cans and petals from flowers and balls from toddlers and anything else it fancied. The market stalls packed up early and the pigeons all vanished and people walked slightly sideways and screwed up their eyes.

Binny, aged twelve, reluctant owner of a dark purple school blazer that looked (though it wasn't) almost like new, was in town with Clem, her seventeen-year-old sister.

It was the last day of the summer break. The next day would be school. Binny so much did not want this to be true that she was busy in her head rewriting the future. She told the improved version to herself like a story.

Lightning zipped . . . zipped or unzipped? Lightning unzipped the sky straight above the Staff Room where all the teachers had rushed to the windows. Not one person escaped the shattering white blast . . . Not cruel, decided Binny. Instant.

Painless, probably. And who would want to be a teacher anyway?

Moments later, the whole school was a great pile of smoldering emb . . .

A star-shaped brightness interrupted Binny, a glowing painted airiness, a butterfly.

Lemon yellow, etched with black. Lapis blue edging on the lower wings, each set with a dusty ruby. Caught and lifted on the air.

It was so different from any butterfly that Binny had ever seen before, so unexpected and so lovely, that she dropped her bag to race after it for a closer look.

"Binny!" screeched Clem.

"Oh!" cried Binny, dodging the traffic but colliding with a passerby. "Oh! Oh, stay!"

It didn't stay. It vanished over the high church wall, gone between one moment and the next, and Binny tumbled back to earth and for the first time saw the results of her collision. A smashed box lay in the gutter, the pavement was scattered with broken flowers, and a voice was shrieking, "LOOK what you've done! Look!"

"I'm sorry . . ."

"Sorry! They're all spoiled! Where's the card? Oh! Move!"

Binny's victim, a dark-haired girl, gave Binny a sudden

furious shove, so hard that she stumbled and fell against the rough stone wall of the churchyard.

"Ruined!" she heard the girl exclaim. "Ruined!"

Shocked into silence, Binny picked herself up and began painfully collecting the flowers.

"Leave them alone! Get out of my way!"

The girl pushed furiously past as Clem arrived on the scene, clutching the blazer bag, grown-up and indignant, exclaiming in wrath, "Binny! You idiot! How utterly insane and stupid! You could have been hit! You could have caused an accident! And that poor girl! All her things!"

Clem's voice made Binny blink, like somebody muddled by magic. She rubbed her eyes, taking in the calamity. "Where's she gone?" she asked.

"She ran off just now. Oh Binny, look!"

It was a birthday card, bent and spoiled, *World's Best Mother* and a pink envelope. Binny's dusty footprint was stamped across the front.

"They were birthday things!" said Clem. "For her mother."

Clem sounded horrified and Binny understood why. All birthdays were important to her sister, but their mother's most of all. While Binny cheerfully handed over a home-made card, a chocolate bar, and a poem of her own composing, Clem saved and planned for something perfect. A special card, a fresh new book, carefully chosen flowers . . .

"I bet that box was a birthday cake," said Clem, retrieving the squashed mess from the gutter. "It was! Look at the ribbon! And she'd bought pink carnations."

"I tried to say sorry," said Binny, grumpy with shame. "She took no notice. *And* she pushed me, twice!"

"No wonder," said Clem.

"She could have waited, instead of just running off."

"She was crying."

"Crying! She wasn't. She was mad, not crying!"

"Crying," said Clem relentlessly. "I should have gone after her. Oh, for goodness' sake, Binny, mop the blood!"

"Blood?"

"Look at your hands!"

Binny looked and saw her knuckles, grazed and oozing crimson. She took the tissues Clem handed her and wound them round like bandages.

"Hurry!" ordered Clem. "Or I'm going home without you. What on earth was it all about anyway?"

"That butterfly! You must have seen!"

"A butterfly! A butterfly! And she lost all her mum's birthday stuff!"

"I'm sorry," said Binny again. "I'm very sorry. I really truly am. But it was honestly an accident. Not like her pushing me. That was on purpose. Is my head bleeding?"

"Your head?"

"Where it hit the wall."

"I didn't know it did. Let me look. Wow! You must have fallen quite hard. There's a huge lump coming! All this trouble because you thought you saw a butterfly!"

"I did see it!" said Binny. "Of course I did! It was huge! Amazing! Gorgeous! A different one from any other I ever saw before. You must have seen it, Clem."

"I saw the traffic," said Clem. "And the girl and all her things spoiled. I can see your hands and your head. I picked up your blazer from where you dropped it . . ."

"Thank you."

" . . . in the middle of the road . . ."

"Sorry."

" . . . but I think you dreamed the butterfly," said Clem.

At home there was no one with time to listen to butterfly stories. There was the next day to plan, new schools in the morning for Binny and her little brother, six-year-old James. College for Clem, and work for their mother, who was coping by making lists.

"Blazer!" she called, the moment Binny and Clem came through the door.

Carefully concealing her wounds, Binny held out the bag.

"Well done!" said her mother, ticking it off. "It was the last thing after James's new shoes. That's the shopping all finished and you ready for tomorrow. Thank goodness!"

"Is James ready too?" asked Clem.

"More or less. I've mended his school bag and scrubbed off all those tattoos and I'm trying to not look at his hair. It's got really long this summer and I seem to have only just noticed."

James's hair was a sun bleached mop. It was shaggy and golden, and people turned to smile at it in the street. Only that morning the shoe shop assistant had remarked, "You would need a heart of stone to cut off hair like that! What a Goldilocks!"

"Binny," James had asked when they were out of the shop. "Did she say 'Goldilocks'? Goldilocks? Like that girl with the bears?"

"She was only joking. You don't even like porridge!"

"And a heart of stone to cut if off?" asked James, squinting at his reflection in a shop window. "What did she mean?"

"She meant it would be hard to do."

It was hard to do, but James's heart was stonier than most. It took him some time to get hold of sharp enough scissors but he had managed it at last. Binny's blazer had just been ticked off the back-to-school list when he walked into the kitchen, shorn and smirking and looking forward to drama.

"Hello! Don't kiss me! Guess who I look like!"

"Hello James, you have been busy," said his mother, unflinchingly crossing *Hair? James?* off her list. "You look like Christopher Robin."

"Christopher Robin! Who's Christopher Robin?" asked James, outraged. "I look like Bart Simpson!"

"They are very alike," said his mother.

"I thought you'd all scream and cry when you saw me!"

"We are screaming and crying inside," said Clem cheerfully.

"Why are we?" asked Binny, who had been peering gloomily into her blazer bag. "What's he done? *Oh no! Oh James!*"

"Yes, that's what *I knew* you'd be like," said James with great satisfaction. "What's for tea?"

"Sausages."

"Just?"

"With chips."

"Beans?"

"Perhaps. What did you do with the cut off hair?"

"I swished it down the drain."

"Disgusting!" said his mother. "Binny, have you bumped your head? And what have you done to your hands?"

"It was a butterfly. I saw it and then I . . . then I banged into a wall! It was a special butterfly; the sort you never see. Clem said I dreamed it, but I didn't. I'm going to call Gareth and ask what kind it was."

"It was the invisible-get-Binny-squashed-on-the-road sort," Clem called after her as she left the room, but Binny took no notice and went off with the phone. Binny and Gareth were a team. Years before, when Binny lost Max, her puppy, it was Gareth who found him and gave him a home. Now Max was shared; school times with Gareth in Oxford, vacations in Cornwall with Binny, and his owners had become friends. Clem had once described them as Fiction and Nonfiction. Gareth was definitely nonfiction, an encyclopedia-reading, bad tempered, naturalist-scientist.

"Of course it didn't 'come out of nowhere'!" he interrupted, as Binny began her description of the butterfly. "And it probably wasn't yellow. Do you mean browny yellow?"

"No," said Binny. "Yellow as yellow! And a cutout sort of shape, with twirly black edges. Big too, and bright! Bright as a picture in a book!"

"A Swallowtail. You couldn't possibly have seen one," said Gareth.

"How could I have told you what it was like if I didn't see it?" Binny demanded.

"You saw a picture somewhere and got mixed up in your head. You're always seeing things. You spent the summer seeing ghosts!"

Binny was suddenly silent.

"And you never know what things are, even when you're looking at them."

"Of course I do!"

"I remember when you used to think seals were fish!"

"That was ages . . ."

"Five and a half weeks," said Gareth, with his usual awful accuracy.

"Oh shut up!"

"Shut up yourself," said Gareth. "It was a Swallowtail but you didn't see it."

It sounded like a quarrel, but it wasn't. Binny and Gareth had an understanding that words could not hurt. It didn't stop them arguing, though.

"I know what I saw and you don't know what I saw," said Binny.

"Why did you ask me, then?"

"I didn't. I just mentioned it. I really wanted to talk to Max."

"Well, that's easy! MAX!" yelled Gareth, and Binny heard

the scurry of paws as Max arrived. He recognized her voice instantly and barked intelligently into the receiver until he was cut off mid woof by Gareth's mother crying in the background that she could not hear herself think.

"You don't get those butterflies in Cornwall," said Gareth, suddenly back again. "Not ever."

"Why not? That doesn't make sense. How would a butterfly know it was Cornwall?"

"What?"

"They have wings. They fly around. So why shouldn't they fly to Cornwall? What's to stop them? They're not going to read the road signs, are they? And think, 'Oh, no! Cornwall! I'm not allowed there!' What sort of butterfly did you say it was?"

"A Swallowtail."

"Have you ever seen one?"

"Yes. In France."

"I've seen one in England," said Binny. "Good-bye!"

"I wish they didn't live in Oxford, a million miles away," she said to her mother, stumping back into the kitchen a minute later. "I wish you'd married Gareth's dad; it would be much easier about Max. Wouldn't you like to? Gareth and me think you still could if you tried."

"Thank you for your confidence but Gareth's father is married to someone else."

"He's only just done it, though."

"It still counts," pointed out Binny's mother. "Although I can see it would be convenient for you. Set the table while you're moaning. How was Gareth?"

"He says I see things that aren't there."

"You two balance each other perfectly!" said her mother. "You see things that aren't there. He doesn't see things that are! Such as his father's extremely nice new wife. When you've done the table, will you go and find James and Clem, please. I sent James to unblock the drain and Clem rushed out for beans but she should be back any minute. Tell them it's suppertime."

There were just four people in the Cornwallis family, the children's mother, Binny, James, and Clem. No grandparents or useful aunts or uncles. Their father was a smiling photograph on the wall of the little sitting room. He had died four years before, leaving behind, like gifts from a wizard: his musical ability for Clem, his love of stories for Binny, and his optimistic self-confidence for James. Binny paused to look at him as she passed. For a long time his eyes had puzzled her, until she realized they were her own. She was gazing at the picture when Clem blew through the door, James's beans in her hand and a gale of wind in her silvery hair.

"Goodness!" she panted. "It's getting wild out there! Hold out your hand, Bin! I caught you a wish! There you are!"

In the Cornwallis family an autumn leaf caught between tree and ground counted for a wish. Clem uncurled her fingers over Binny's palm to give her a birch leaf, butterfly yellow and butterscotch brown.

"Save it for an emergency," said Clem.

Binny held the leaf carefully, cradling it in her hand so that it shouldn't be bent.

"Thank you," she said, so solemnly that Clem laughed and said, "You may never need it!"

"I think I will," said Binny.

Summer 1912, Part 1

There were three of them. Rupert, who was the eldest, and his cousins, thirteen-year-old Peter and Clarry, who was ten. Their mothers had been sisters and their fathers were brothers and every year since Clarry could remember, she and Peter had spent the summer at the house in Cornwall, where Rupert lived with their grandparents. The grandparents seemed to have very little to do with this arrangement. In the term time Rupert was sent to boarding school. During vacations they provided beds and meals and closed the sitting room door.

"They don't fuss," said the boys with satisfaction. "Wash it well," they would say at the sight of a cut knee. "Do stop," at the advent of tears. Only illness surprised them. "You can't have measles!" they told Clarry the summer that she was eight. Clarry had measles anyway, all by herself in the bedroom overlooking the garden. Now and then people brought her drinks and told her what day it was. It was extremely uncomfortable and boring and lonely and sometimes she wondered if a little fussing would be as bad as the boys seemed to believe. It didn't happen, so she never found out.

Rupe, who was hardly ever called Rupert, had been going to boarding school for years. Nothing could frighten him. Clarry and Peter lived in Plymouth with their father. He was perpetually busy, but he was not unkind and he paid their train fares to their grandparents' house with no complaints at all. He always saw them off from the station, with new hats and books, and apples for the journey. Once he even remembered Clarry's birthday and added a present, a silver box with a comb and hairbrush and looking glass inside, but Clarry did not usually have birthdays because the day she was born her mother had died. ("Thank you very much," Peter had said bitterly, when he informed her of this fact, and Clarry, stabbed to the heart with guilt, had thought, Oh Peter! Oh, poor Peter. I must look after Peter.)

For Clarry, there could have been no better way to spend her birthday than summer with Rupe and Peter at their grandparents' house. It seemed to her that each was better than the one before. The brightness of those summers illuminated the whole year for Clarry. The glow of the one that had passed did not fade until the shimmer of the one ahead could be seen on the horizon.

The house was in the country and the grandparents believed the countryside to be safe. Clarry, Rupe, and Peter were allowed to do exactly as they liked. They lost themselves on the moors, poisoned themselves with toadstools, were chased by bullocks, stung by wasps, and tumbled from trees and walls and rock faces. Clarry nearly drowned when the boys taught her to swim by abandoning her in deep water. Rupe was ill for three days after picking up, and being bitten by, a baby adder. When Peter was twelve he jumped from the train that ran through the dark cutting beyond the end of the garden.

This broke his leg.

Peter's broken leg was the start of the museum.

Chapter Two

The last of the shopping was done. The last summer break supper eaten and cleared away. Clem, who dealt with stress by organization, had run out of things to tidy.

"I think we're really truly ready at last!" said the children's mother, and James, shorn like a lamb and fueled by sausages, turned an exuberant somersault over the end of the sofa. He landed on Clem, who tipped him onto the floor beside Cinderella the cat.

"You should be in bed," she told him, and although James pleaded, "Not yet! Not yet!" the words had been said, and the last day of the summer was over.

Binny went upstairs feeling chilly with dread. In the morning she would have to face the new school. They had only moved to the town at the beginning of the summer break. She wouldn't know a single person.

Clem was good at making friends and James bounced up to people as if he had known them all his life. But Binny could not do those things; she didn't shine like Clem or glow like James. She was clumsy and defensive and she said things that sounded terrible.

However, she was brave. In the morning she got up and put on the new gray and purple uniform without any fuss.

"I know how I look, so don't say anything," she announced when she came downstairs. "Worse than I've ever looked in my life and don't try and cheer me up."

"I've seen you looking much worsener than that," said James at once. "Often!"

"You've forgotten the year all your front teeth fell out at the same time," added Clem.

"That uniform isn't really much worse than the chopped off old jeans you've been running around in all summer," said her mother. "Anyway, you'll all look the same when you get there."

"You should come to my school." James dug deep holes in a jar of chocolate spread as he spoke. "Then you could look like me!" He loved his cheerful red sweatshirt and red baseball cap. His new vertical hair stuck out around the cap like dandelion petals.

"Wow!" he said when he looked in the mirror before he set off to school. "Just *wow*! Come on, Binny!"

But Binny would not come. She went off to school alone.

"Won't you walk with me and James?" asked her mother. "Just for the first day? Your schools are almost next door to each other."

"No, because then everyone would say, 'That's the girl who gets taken to school with her mum and her little brother!'" answered Binny. She left them without looking back and all the way to school her legs felt strange and heavy, as if she was walking in a dream.

But at the end of the day, on the way home again, Binny ran.

She couldn't help it. She began by walking very fast, but soon the need to get away was so great that she gave in and sprinted. Through the town she ran, across the star shaped marketplace where tree-loads of wishes were tumbling in the wind, and onto the narrow street that led uphill to their house.

Home came in glimpses to meet her. Cinderella disappearing behind a dustbin. The flower tub full of white geraniums. Two granite steps and the small blue painted door with a dolphin shaped knocker.

Binny drew a deep breath and pushed the door open.

The radio in the kitchen competed with the cuckoo clock on the stairs. Clem's flute repeated a phrase, over and over. Binny stepped over James's new school shoes, dropped her bag on the doormat, and was safe.

In the kitchen her mother was peeling apples.

"Binny!" she exclaimed, putting down an apple to hug her. "How are you? Come and tell me! What was it like?"

Like? thought Binny. She could find no words. How to describe the day of bewilderment, buffeting, trouble, and scorn? She stared speechlessly up at her mother.

"Binny?"

An idea came to Binny, bright as a switched-on light. A wonderful solution, if only her mother would see it.

"Actually Mum, I'm really sorry but I didn't seem to learn anything. It's not a very good school, everyone says."

"Binny, what went wrong?"

"Nothing. Absolutely nothing! I just thought, what about if I get books from the library and teach myself at home?"

"It's only been one day, Bin."

"I know," said Binny earnestly. "I only said it because if we want to sell my uniform it would be better to do it now, before I've worn it very much. I was only being sensible, like you always say! I could look after Cinderella while you're at work. And I could teach James as well! Easily! Then he needn't go to school either."

"But . . ."

"Please don't say 'but'!" begged Binny.

"Oh Binny!"

"Think how much I'd know if I just read all the books in the library! I could do that. You always like me going to the library!"

"That's true. I do. I love you going to the library."

Binny's mother picked up another apple and began peeling very carefully. Binny waited. Was she going to say, "All right Binny. Take off your uniform and put it in a bag to sell! Of course you can stay at home and teach yourself with library books."

No, she wasn't. There was a two-apple-long pause, and then she said, very quietly and carefully, "Binny, remember how you didn't like your old school at first?"

"I didn't say I didn't like this new school," said Binny. "I just said it wasn't very good."

"Yes, I see."

Binny reached for a piece of apple peel and ate it, wincing at the sourness.

"Did you have a nice lunch?"

"Not really. Lettuce."

"Just lettuce?"

"Well, bits of tomato and cucumber and stuff."

"What sort of stuff?"

"Cheese."

"Anything else?"

"Well, fries," admitted Binny. "But no pudding. Only a milk shake."

"I made flapjacks," said her mother, kindly not saying that cheese salad and fries and a milk shake would have pleased Binny at any other time. "Would you like some? And you could take some to James as well."

"Where is he?"

"He went off to do his homework."

"Homework? James?"

It was true. Binny found him lying on his bedroom floor coloring a picture of a pirate. Beside him lay his loot from his first day at school: a reading book, a party invitation, and somebody else's hat.

"Hi James!"

"Hello, don't kiss me," said James, the precaution he had taken with his family ever since he learned to speak.

"Fancy giving you homework on your first day!" said Binny. "What an awful school. Poor you. Would you like to leave and stay home with me instead?"

"No I wouldn't!" said James ungratefully. "We're doing pirates in history and there's a climbing frame and two slides in the playground and I'm a monitor. Your shadow is going all over my homework."

Binny moved her shadow.

"Do you know what a monitor is?" continued James, busily giving his pirate a dripping red sword. "They're the most important ones, after the teacher. They do messages to the office, walking not running. Because what would it be like if everyone ran? I walk," he said virtuously, "even when no one's looking. Guess what everyone calls me? 007! That's good, isn't it?"

"I suppose," admitted Binny. "So do you like your school, then?"

"I *love* it!" said James.

"Aren't you going to ask if I like mine?"

"Do you?"

"No."

James colored for a minute longer and then murmured, "Binny."

"What?"

"Your shadow."

Clem was more comforting. She groaned when Binny showed her that the gray and purple blazer had someone else's name tag inside.

"I didn't mind that it was from the nearly new shop," said Binny. "But I didn't want anyone else to know."

"Give it to me! Let me look!" said Clem, holding out her hand. "We should have checked. I never thought of it. Nobody will have noticed, though, Bin."

"The whole class noticed," said Binny. "Because I left it behind by accident and somebody took it to the office and they gave it back to the wrong person. A fat girl in the year above. And I don't talk posh, do I Clem?"

"You?"

"I knew I didn't. They say I do. They said that's how they knew I was a grockle."

"A what?"

"It's someone who shouldn't be here," said Binny. "Someone from away. They notice when people are from away. They say, 'You're not from round here, are you?'"

Clem didn't argue. She had been asked that question herself that day, at least a dozen times.

"There was every sort of person at my old school," Binny went on. "Scruffy and posh. From loads of different places. Nobody said grockle. But the worst thing was much worse than that! You know that girl who dropped her things in the street when I saw the butterfly? She was there!"

"Binny! I hope you said sorry to her properly this time!

Straightaway! Did you? And asked how you could make up? Binny? Bin?"

"Not straightaway."

Clem groaned.

"I hoped she wouldn't recognize me!" said Binny. "I don't look like me in this uniform, do I? I just look like anyone from anywhere! Like Mum said, we all look the same! But she knew it was me straightaway."

Clem looked at Binny's unique seaweed bunchy hair, stubborn chin, wide green eyes, and church wall bruise in the middle of her forehead and said, "Of course she knew it was you!"

"Clem, don't you think it was awful bad luck her being there?"

"Where else would she be?" asked Clem. "This is a really small town. One school, one college. You meet the same people over and over. You'd better tell me what happened."

"It wasn't my fault. As soon as I saw her I ducked out of the way . . ."

"Ducked out of the way?"

"So I could think what to do. I thought it would be better to make friends with her when a few days had gone . . ."

"This is appalling!" said Clem.

"I was going to be really kind to make up, and then

when she got used to me *of course* I was going to say sorry! But she knew it was me straightaway. She said, 'It was you!' and I said, 'What was me?' . . ."

"Binny!"

"And then she told everyone that I smashed up her mum's birthday flowers and squashed her mum's birthday cake and trampled on her mum's birthday card. I said sorry. I said it about a million times. A million million."

"A bit too late!" said Clem.

"It wasn't! It didn't make any difference. She wouldn't listen and she made it sound as if I'd done it on purpose. She's called Clare and she's got a friend called Ella. She's horrible too. She said, 'Why do you call yourself Binny? Binny's not a name!' So I said, 'It's actually Belinda,' and then they both started saying, *'Is it, actually?'* and *'Actually, it is!'* They thought they were so funny. I'm going to leave that rubbish school. I told them so, and they said 'Good!'"

"School will soon get used to you, Binny, and you'll get used to them."

"I won't. I hate them all."

"You don't really," said Clem, who was used to Binny, with her loves and her hates, her fears and her courage, her dark and her light. "I've taken that name out of the blazer and put in yours instead. If I were you I'd get a card for

Clare and write inside how sorry you are and how you were too embarrassed to say so when you met her . . ."

"She didn't say sorry to me! She didn't say one word about pushing me into the wall!"

"Binny, do you want this to be over, or not?"

"It would be much easier just to leave school," said Binny, but Clem said not to be daft and that one day soon all the fuss would be forgotten.

"Promise!" said Clem, but Binny could not believe this. She could only see a future of being the enemy, labeled a grockle, of being told she talked posh, of lonely pretended interest in alien notice boards.

Unbearable.

That night, when Binny went up to her tiny cupboard of a bedroom, she caught sight of something small and bright on the windowsill. A birch leaf. Clem's wishing leaf.

"I wish," said Binny aloud, "that something would happen to stop it being school in the morning."

"Wake up! Wake up! Come on, Binny, sit up!"

"Go away!" moaned Binny.

"Quick! Hurry! Clem's already downstairs with James."

A flashlight beam bounced around the room showing

a black liquid window. Binny's scrapbook-pictured walls seemed to rustle and flutter. There was a watery sound.

"It's not morning and it's not funny," groaned Binny, and burrowed back under her quilt.

It was snatched from her. The watery sound increased to a pouring rush. The flashlight beam ricocheted from the mirror as her mother pulled her out of bed. They both just made it to the doorway before a huge chunk of ceiling fell.

"Why? Why? Why?" demanded Binny as she stumbled and shivered down the narrow cottage stairs. "What did it? Was it James? Why can't we have the lights on?"

"The power's off," explained her mother. "It's a storm. We must have a hole in the roof. No, James, you are *not* going outside!"

"But my chickens!" wailed James.

They had been his wonderful surprise present from the old people at the home where his mother worked. Pecker and Gertie, two brown hens.

"Pecker! Gertie!" roared James.

"They'll be all right. They've got a nice strong roof. It's not safe to go out just yet. Listen!"

Louder than the wind, harder than the rattle of the rain that flung itself against the windows, was the sound of roof tiles crashing to the ground.

"I've got Cinderella," said Clem. "I've put her in her traveling basket in case we need to leave."

Clem was calm in this emergency, collecting coats and bags ready to be grabbed, fielding Binny from the windows and James from the doors.

"What if the walls blow down?" asked Binny, fearfully. "What'll we do? We've only just moved here!"

"This house has been here more than three hundred years," said her mother. "The walls won't blow down. Wrap your quilt around you and curl up on the sofa until it gets light. You too, Clem. And James can have the big chair. Try and get some sleep."

"What about you?" asked Binny.

"I'll take care of Cinderella. Come on James, I've made a little tent for you."

James crawled into his little tent, stayed still for one moment, and then exploded through the blanket walls, crying in anguish. "MY HOMEWORK! It's in my bed- room and I need it for school tomorrow!"

It was then that a great sunny warmth seemed to pour over Binny.

"You needn't worry about that, James," she said. "There's definitely not going to be any school in the morning!"

Summer 1912, Part 2

The museum was Peter's idea to begin with, although he was soon joined by Rupert. It was stocked, arranged, and owned by the boys. At first Clarry was not involved at all.

"She can visit, though, I suppose," said Peter. The boys often talked about Clarry as if she wasn't there.

"I'm in the room!" said Clarry.

"She should visit," agreed Rupe. "She might learn something."

"I'm *in* the *room*!"

"Did you hear anything just then, Pete?"

"No."

"Thought something squeaked."

Clarry marched out of the room, found some nails and a hammer, and started an art gallery on the landing. It failed within hours when the grandparents noticed the clean pale oblongs on the walls downstairs, and came up and reclaimed their property. The grandparents didn't like the nail holes either; Clarry had used large nails, and plenty of them. The grandparents' complaints were so bitter that the proprietor of the gallery ran away to the end of the garden, where she climbed onto the wall and chopped off all her hair.

"Why?" asked Rupert when he finally managed to track her down.

"I just did," said Clarry, holding her raggy dark head very high in the air.

"First Pete jumps out of a train. Then you cut your hair off. My turn next. I'll have to look for another adder. Now come on down, Clarry, I've got you a job."

Clarry looked at Rupe doubtfully, suspecting more teasing.

"What job?" she asked.

"This museum of Pete's. He's taking it very seriously. He wants everything organized and labeled, he says. You've always liked fiddling about with stuff like that, haven't you?"

"Like what?" Clarry still showed no signs of climbing down from the wall.

"Indian ink and fancy writing, like in a real museum. Pete said you'd be perfect."

"Peter said that?"

"Said you'd do it properly," said Rupe, not mentioning the difficulty with which he had dragged these words from Peter.

Clarry, who was not used to praise, especially from her brother, was still cautious. "Why didn't he ask me himself?"

"He's stuck upstairs with a busted leg, isn't he? Poor old Pete, it's not his fault that he's wrecked for the summer."

"He jumped off a *train* onto *rocks*!"

"I like your hair."

"Do I look like a boy?"

"No. Come on."

Clarry's writing was her best thing, clear and fine, like the marks on a shell, or the lines on the wings of certain butterflies. Very carefully she wrote:

Cast Skin of Grass Snake
(*Natrix natrix*)
July 1912

Found by Rupert Penrose
amongst the reeds beside the river

"Not that bit about Rupe," objected Peter.

"It makes it more interesting," said Clarry.

"It's not the sort of thing we need. It's not as if we are going to forget."

"But in a hundred years' time," said Clarry, "when some-body is looking at the things and wondering . . ."

Peter snorted.

"Put it on the back of the card," suggested Rupe, and after a minute or two of arguing, this was agreed upon.

"In case she rushes away and cuts off any more hair," said Peter.

Skull and wing feathers of male Kestrel
(*Falco tinnunculus*)
July 1912

Found by Clarry Penrose on the tideline
(but Rupe picked it up)

"Does it matter who picked it up?" asked Peter.

"Well, she wasn't going to," said Rupe.

"I noticed it, though," said Clarry. "I saw it first!" She was proud of the kestrel skull, and once she had got used to it the horror faded from the empty eye sockets and thin stained bone. "It's beautiful," she said. On a blank museum card she drew the fragile curves and the small hooked beak, and wondered how it had come to be there on the edge of the sea amongst the bladder wrack and empty mermaids' purses.

★ ★ ★

The museum was a wandering institution: It started off in Peter's room, because his broken leg fixed him there. Then, when he was well enough to hop, it moved to the dining room, which was so cold that it was hardly ever used. It stayed there until the smell (some seashells and a mole that no one had quite summoned the courage to stuff) penetrated to the more inhabited parts of the house. After that it moved to a cobwebby outhouse, where it remained for the rest of the summer.

"It ought to have a name," said Clarry. "We could paint it on a signboard and put it on the door. THE MUSEUM OF THE PENROSE COUSINS. What about that?"

"Inside would there just be me and you and Peter?" asked Rupe, laughing. "All neatly labeled and sitting on a shelf?"

"I didn't mean that!" protested Clarry. "You know I didn't! I just thought it would be nice."

"Nice!" said Peter scornfully.

Clarry said no more about a notice on the door but later that day, carefully lettering a card for a very large cobweb that filled a window corner, she remembered her idea.

Web of Common House spider
(*Tegenaria domestica*)
August 1912

wrote Clarry on the front and she added on the back:

The Museum of the Penrose Cousins
A World Famous Collection from All Over the World
Collected by
Rupert Penrose
Peter Penrose
Clarry Penrose

Clarry nodded with satisfaction. It does look nice, she thought.

Once the museum was established in the outhouse Peter tackled the mole. He sat at the window shelf and worked with his pocketknife, his face very determined, his too long hair in his eyes. Rupe watched critically, with his hands in his pockets.

"You might help him, Rupe!" said Clarry from the doorway (she wouldn't come farther) and Peter, knowing he was being pitied, gave her one of his furious glances, bent closer, jerked harder, and after an unpleasant interval which Clarry could not watch, succeeded in separating the mole from its skin. Or most of the mole from most of its skin, as Rupe pointed out.

The other exhibits were less shatteringly biological. Fossils, feathers, crystals. An antler from a roe deer, a wasp's nest, a butterfly.

Small Tortoiseshell
(*Aglais urtica*)
September 1912

Last day of the summer vacation

Chapter Three

Binny loved the storm. The little sitting room was like a cave, and the wind outside was a wild friendly beast, a wolf or a tame dragon, defending her from the perils of the day to come. Curled up on the sofa she dozed and woke and dozed again, comforted by the racket and the warmth of Clem, drowsing beside her. By daylight the worst of the gale was over. Tiles stopped falling, the rain ended at last, and the power came back again. With the return of power came the lovely news that all the schools were closed.

"That was a brilliant wishing leaf you gave me, Clem!" said Binny.

As soon as the rain stopped, the indignant population of the town emerged to look at the damage. Everywhere were broken branches, flattened fences, tumbled chimney pots and torn roofs.

"Our house," said James proudly, "is one of the worst!"

It was true. There were two great holes in the roof. From Binny's room and from the bathroom they could look straight up into the sky. So much rain had poured in that the bedroom ceilings had either fallen completely or hung low and menacing, like great sagging clouds. There was a terrible smell of oldness and wetness. Many things were ruined, although James's homework was discovered safe and only slightly damp under his pillow, and out in the garden Gertie and Pecker were found not only to be safe, but also to have produced two warm brown eggs.

"Two!" said James. "They've never done that before, not two." He gloated, an egg in each hand, like an unexpected millionaire, and his only worries were those of all unexpected millionaires: "Shall I have to share?"

"'Course not," said Binny, who was out in the garden with him. "Your chickens, your eggs!"

"What do you think made them do it? Was it because the roof blew off?"

"Bet it was," said Binny.

"Fantastic, then!" said James, looking around at the devastation, and Binny completely agreed.

"I bet it will take ages to mend," she said, and borrowed the family cell phone to send Gareth an extremely gloating text:

AMAZING STORM! ROOF BLOWN OFF!
NO MORE SCHOOL! HOPE YOU HAVEN'T
2 MUCH HOMEWORK BINNY

and she got one back almost straightaway saying

DON'T SEND ME MESSAGES IN MATH! GARETH

"Math!" she told James. "Poor old Gareth is doing math!"

"We do math at my school," said James. "We did it yester-day. In blue books, drawing things, like nine apples in the bowl and the other half of the rabbit."

"Well, you've escaped now."

"I got a star. Green. For my Star Card. Are we going to have to live in the garden?"

Binny had been so pleased to have school put safely out of the question that she had not thought of the prob-lems that having no roof would cause. No one but James seemed to have done either. Their mother was next door, making urgent phone calls from their neighbors' much-less-damaged house, but Clem was inside, emptying the fridge into a cooler. Binny went in to see her.

"James says, 'Are we going to have to live in the garden?'" she said.

"I'm not!" said Clem decisively.

"So what will we do?"

"Something," said Clem, "and definitely not living in the garden!"

"I've got these eggs," said James, appearing beside Binny. "Where shall I put them to be safe? I can't keep carrying around eggs and eggs and eggs." James yawned; it had been a long night. "What next?" he asked. "Something's got to happen next," he said.

James was right. By the end of the day, bright blue tarpaulin had been spread over the broken roof. Clothes had been retrieved and packed. A friend of a friend knew of a house on the other side of town. It was rented in summer to holidaymakers. It was empty. It would do.

All in one exhausting afternoon, they moved house.

"Thank goodness that I bought a car!" said the children's mother. She nearly hadn't—they had managed for years without one, only the weight of shopping had persuaded her to do it—but now it was necessary. It took three trips, including the chickens, who didn't enjoy it at all.

After the narrow friendly streets of town, this new temporary home seemed a bare sort of place, especially to the Cornwallis family, city people all their lives. It stood on a road that was so deep in trees that the buildings were lost amongst them. On one side were fields of scrubby grass. On the other, farther along, was a farm. Even Binny, still giddy with relief at the success of her wishing leaf, said "Oh," at her first sight of their new home. When she had climbed so cheerfully into the car she had not imagined quite such a chilly ending to the journey. The house was tall, and granite gray, with high, cold chimneys and empty windows. A long, wild garden stretched out behind, and a steep slope led down to a disused railway line.

The family were peering into the windows when the woman who owned it appeared to show them round.

From the very beginning she seemed to not quite trust them.

"There was no wind here that would have taken off a roof," she said. "Not a *roof*! A few tiles maybe. I did hear of people who lost a tile or so, but a *roof . . .*"

"The rain made it so much worse," explained the children's mother.

"Oh, rain!" said the woman, as if surprised to hear of such a thing. "Well. You'd better come in."

They found themselves in a place of large bare rooms with high ceilings and heavy, old-fashioned furniture. There were also unwelcoming locked doors.

"When we started renting the house out we locked the good furniture in that back room," the woman explained. "The attic is locked too, and the key's gone missing but you'd have no call to be up there anyway. There's nothing to see but junk. The cupboards I must keep fastened or I have all the cleaning stuff used. People will meddle, especially when the weather's not good for the beach. Children meddle," she added, giving James a look.

James, who certainly was a champion meddler, smiled serenely back at her. Binny glanced up at the woman, wondering if she guessed how little he could be relied on to leave a locked door locked. Already she didn't like this determined, uneasy woman, but she had to admit that she was probably right about James.

"It's not forever," said the children's mother, when they were finally alone. "And it's not really so far from everywhere. It only feels like it because of the long road and all the trees."

"And no streetlights," said Clem.

"Aren't there?"

"No. I noticed. It's going to be really dark at night."

They both looked anxiously at Binny.

"It'll be exciting," said Binny. In her mind, school was receding further and further into impossibility. No streetlights just added to the remoteness. "Like in the old days," she added cheerfully. "A hundred years ago. When nobody went to school."

"I think you'll find they did," said her mother, but Binny shook her head as if to scatter away such an idea and went to look for James. She found him peering through the keyhole of the locked back room. He jumped guiltily at her approach and began, "Hello, don't kiss . . ."

"When did I ever?" demanded Binny. "When did anyone ever?"

"People have," said James, rubbing his cheek as if those unwanted kisses still lingered. "I can't see anything through this little hole."

"Let me try."

They took turns peering at lumpy dark shadows until their mother called, "Binny! James!" She set them to finding supper for everyone while she and Clem made beds and searched for the central heating switch, which did not exist because there was no central heating.

"Who needs heating in September!" said the children's mother, but the evening was cold and the sight of Cinderella, stalking disconsolately through the unwelcoming rooms, did not make it feel any warmer.

"Poor Cinderella!" said Cinderella's family, bravely not

saying, "Poor us." They were glad when it was time to eat Binny and James's supper: hot chocolate, hot soup, toasted cheese, and chocolate cookies.

"It was just about this time yesterday that you gave me that leaf!" remarked Binny to Clem as they washed the dishes together afterward. "What's that?"

It was a sudden rattle at the back door and there stood their landlady again. She held a bottle of wine, a spare door key, and four hot water bottles. These things she dumped on the kitchen table as if they were insults she'd forgotten to give the first time round. She ignored the chorus of thanks.

"You said pet. I thought dog. I didn't know you were bringing a cat," she said, catching sight of Cinderella. "White. The hair will get everywhere. However. What can I hear?"

It was a sound from above. The merry bong of bed-springs. James, trying out the beds.

"James!" called his mother crossly.

"I should have thought you'd had enough," remarked the woman rather grimly, "of ceilings coming down!"

"You're absolutely right!" agreed the children's mother, and shouted again, "James! Stop that at once!"

Bong! went another bounce and Clem turned, whisked upstairs, and brought James down by the scruff of his neck.

"Oh, you've come back!" said James, looking at the woman with interest. "Are you going to live here too? That'll be weird."

"James, you know you are not allowed to jump on beds," his mother told him severely. "Not at home, and not here."

"I didn't know about not here," said James. "Where am I allowed to do it, then?"

"Nowhere, and please say sorry!"

"Sorry," said James, and the woman said, "Yes," and then added, "You might find it useful to know buses go into town every hour on the hour from the end of our road. And back on the half."

"Half road?" asked James. "Or half bus?"

Clem took him away again.

"How useful about the buses," said the children's mother. "That will be such a help! We really do appreciate you taking us in so quickly. And James won't be jumping on the beds again."

"He's only six," explained Binny, making the all-too-often used family excuse for James.

"Old enough," said the woman. "Well. Good night."

She was gone at last.

"Old enough for what?" asked Binny.

"And who *is* she?" demanded Clem, reappearing the

moment the door was closed. "We don't even know her name!"

"I know," agreed her mother. "It's so awkward. I must find out as soon as I can. We're renting through an agency and she didn't introduce herself. What have you done with awful James?"

"He wanted to play hide-and-seek so I counted to a hundred and then came away and left him."

"What a brilliant idea!" exclaimed Binny. "Where is he?"

"Top shelf of the linen closet."

"James! James!" called Binny, dashing up the stairs. "Come on! I've found you! Now you count for me! Let's go outside."

"*Not* outside!" called her mother, but too late, Binny had pulled the door open. There was a smell of damp autumn air, a squawk in the gray twilight, and a rustle on the door-step. Then Pecker appeared, all in a rush, right into the kitchen with all her feathers flurried.

"Pecker!" exclaimed Binny.

"Pecker?" echoed James, coming into the kitchen.

Pecker flapped with difficulty up onto the kitchen table, scattering knives and spoons. She pecked at a hot water bottle in a distracted kind of way.

The family stared and said, "But, Pecker!" puzzled, pleased to see her, moving the wine before it was knocked off the table.

"See if you can pick her up without frightening her," said the children's mother. "James. James?"

But James was not there.

They found him in the garden, shouting in the dark. "Gertie! Gertie!"

"Has Gertie escaped too?" asked his mother. "Binny, I saw a flashlight in one of the kitchen drawers. See if you can find it!"

Binny ran back into the house. She heard Clem say, "Don't worry, James, she won't have gone far!" and her mother call, "James, come down from that wall!" Then she heard James cry, "It's gone! It's gone! Gertie!" She found the flashlight, grabbed it, and rushed back out again.

"Give it to me!" begged James, and shone the flashlight on bushes and trees, and the old stone wall, and then the overturned hen run and long autumn grass.

Rusty orange feathers were caught in the grass.

"Look what it did!" wailed James.

"What did? What are you talking about? What did you see?"

"It ran off with Gertie! Like a dog, only it wasn't a dog . . ."

"Oh no! A fox!"

"It went over the wall with Gertie flapping. She was trying to fly. Come on!"

"No, James!" His mother caught him as he ran. "Not now. Not in the dark."

"Yes," insisted James, who was accustomed to being obeyed, but his mother's grip only got tighter, and after a short struggle he was taken indoors, given hot chocolate and toast, and allowed to call out of the kitchen window. "Gertie! Gertie! Come back!"

But Gertie didn't come back.

By bedtime James had a name for Gertie's capturer.

"A jagular," he said.

"I don't think so," said his mother, hugging him. "I don't think I've ever heard of jaguars in England."

"You didn't listen!" said James, wriggling free from her arms. "Jagu*lars! Lars! Lars! Lars!* Like on TV!"

"There's polar bears on TV," said Clem, laughing. "Polar bears and jaguars! You're mixing them up!"

"It's not funny!" roared James, tired and cross and unhappy, and for about the tenth time that evening, he opened the door and peered into the garden.

"I bet we find her perfectly safe in the morning," said Binny, coming to stand beside him. "She might easily have got away."

"Might she?"

"Think how fierce she was when you tried to get an egg she had laid!"

James looked at his small brown hands, which had suffered many indignant beaky jabs, and nodded.

"And her feet!" said Binny. "When she kicked. Like talons!"

"Binny!" interrupted her mother, meaning, *Do not let James hope things that cannot be true.*

Binny said no more. James closed the door and sighed. Clem hugged him as she went past carrying the hot water bottles to take the chill off the beds upstairs. The children's mother unpacked and unpacked and unpacked. Despite all that had happened, Binny felt smooth with peace. She listened to the wind outside and asked, "What makes it blow?"

"Leaves," said James.

"How?"

"They flap it." He pulled open a drawer beneath a cupboard, found a piece of ancient card, and flapped it in Binny's face. "Like that," he explained. "Like Gertie's wings." Very soon afterward he fell asleep with his head on the table.

His family looked at him regretfully. He would have to be woken, and he would be awful when he was.

"We can't leave him there, though," said his mother bravely. "Come on, James, bedtime!"

"Get off! Not now!" James flailed at his attackers as they carried him away. "Let me stay where I *was*! I want my *old* toothbrush! I don't like blue toothpaste, that towel smells funny, my pillow feels *awful*, I can tuck myself up. Don't laugh and *don't kiss me*!"

"Phew!" said everyone when he was finally disposed of for the night.

"We'll all go to bed," said the children's mother. "I'll just tidy the kitchen and see Pecker is safe. Poor Pecker. Poor Gertie. Off you go and get ready, Binny, then you can listen out for James for me while I'm downstairs."

Binny always enjoyed the adventure of going to bed in a new place. She opened the long narrow window to listen to the wind. It billowed the curtains and lifted her heart and smelled of smoke and leaves and rain.

James was fast asleep when she peeped round his door a few minutes later, sprawled over his pillow like a red and white pajama–striped star. He looked like he hadn't a sorrow in the world, but deep in the night Binny heard him crying.

Never, ever, could Binny resist James's rare tears. She crept into his room and knelt by his bed to comfort him.

"Hullo," hiccupped James. "Don't k . . . k . . ."

"It's all right, I won't."

"Gertie!" said James.

"We might find her in the morning."

"Do you bet we will, or bet we won't?"

Binny drew a deep breath.

"Won't," said James, and did not resist Binny's hand when she rubbed him between his small shaking shoulder blades.

"I'll look for her," promised Binny. "I'm good at looking for things. Remember how I found Max? No one could have been more lost than Max."

"Yes." James gave one last great gulp and turned his face into his pillow. Binny patted his back, the way they had done when he was much smaller, and needed to be patted to sleep. He allowed the patting as he had allowed the rubbing.

"Binny? Bin . . . ?"

"I'm still here."

James said something, all blurry into his damp pillow. "I love you."

Why did she argue with him? Binny wondered. Laugh at him? Think it was a good idea to leave him on the top shelf of the linen closet? The light from the landing shone dimly in at the doorway. It made smooth feathers of his hair and curved shadows of his eyelashes. He was enchanting. Perfect. How odd that she had never realized before.

"I'll look and look," she whispered. "I'll start tomorrow."

"Mmmm," murmured James, and he slept more deeply.

Summer 1913, Part 1

Even before the train had quite stopped, Peter and Clarry were worried.

"He's not here," said Peter, already at the carriage door, and Clarry, crowding against him to see out of the grimy window, said, "He must be! He promised! Who's that running over the bridge?"

"Someone else completely."

"Oh. Oh yes. But they're looking this way." Clarry leaned past him to wave, just in case.

"Stop it!" snapped Peter, shoving her aside. "There's people waiting to get on! Move out of the way!" Clumsily he pulled open the door and climbed down onto the familiar platform.

"Pass me the bags!" he ordered.

"Peter, turn round and look! I'm sure that person is waving to us."

"The bags!" repeated Peter. "Come on! Where's the coats? You've left them on the seat! Oh, let me past!"

Peter clambered up the step again and hurried back to the carriage. He returned in time to hear Clarry give a small squeal. "Peter!" she said. "It is! It's Rupe! It really is!"

"It can't be," said Peter, staring blankly over his burden of coats at the stranger hurrying toward them, but it was.

"Hello kids!"

For a moment Clarry was utterly silent. Rupe, six inches taller, with a new voice. Also a summer blazer, long white flannel trousers, and . . .

"A hat!" said Clarry.

Rupe slowly closed one eye, tipped his hat to Clarry, and pretended to reel backward when she flung herself upon him.

"Rupe! Rupe! We couldn't even tell it was you! Peter said . . ."

Peter rammed her hard with the corner of his bag.

"Can you manage there, Peter?" asked Rupe, disentangling himself, tucking Clarry's hand under one arm and scooping up her bag with the other. "What did he say, Clarry?"

"He said you were someone else completely!"

Rupe grinned.

"I was joking!" snapped Peter furiously. "She never understands."

"You haven't changed a bit!" Rupe told him. "Poor old Peter! Hurry up, I've got Lucy with the trap."

"You came with Lucy on your own?"

"Why not? There she is!"

The small boy who was holding the pony's bridle let go and stepped back as Clarry unhooked herself from Rupe and ran to put her arms around Lucy's satin neck. "Lucy, Lucy, Lucy," she murmured, and breathed the sweet warm pony smell.

"Same old Clarry," said Rupe.

"I know," said Peter crossly. "And I have to lug her around with me everywhere I go!"

"I wouldn't mind."

"You've changed. You'd have minded last year!" Peter suddenly shoved his armload of coats into Rupe's arms, pushed past him, and dived into the station flower bed.

"I told him he'd have to do that," said Clarry, looking at her brother's heaving back, and wincing for the flowers. "It's the only way to get better. He's been holding it in since Plymouth. Had I better go and hold his head?"

"I think he's managing quite nicely on his own," said Rupe, grinning.

"It's why he's been so nasty. And then seeing you. When he's only got knickerbockers."

"Shush!"

"When did they let you have long ones? When did they let you start driving Lucy? When did your voice go like that?"

"Did you expect me to stay twittering like a swallow forever?"

"Yes," said Clarry, and Rupe laughed. Even his laugh was different from the summer before, but he was nice to Peter when he finally emerged from the splattered fuchsia bushes, calling him Pete, and telling him that his bicycle, sent on in advance, had already arrived.

"The chain was off, so I shoved it on again. I hope that was right?" asked Rupe, as if Peter was the expert.

"Thanks," mumbled Peter, thawing a little.

"Your busted leg all right again now?"

"What? Yes fine. Bit stiff."

"You must have a whacking great scar," said Rupe, which was clever of him because Peter did, and took a bleak sort of pleasure in startling people with it.

"Nothing much," he muttered.

"Nothing much!" exclaimed Clarry from her seat behind the boy in the pony trap. "It's enormous! It looks like someone tried to cut his leg off with a wobbly knife. Show Rupe, Peter!"

"He doesn't want to see it."

"Yes I do," said Rupe. "Go on, show me! I promise not to faint!"

"Oh all right," said Peter, and rolled down the top of his stocking. Rupe peered over and whistled with shock, and Peter had to turn his face away, in case anyone saw how pleased he was.

"Is it as bad as you thought it would be?" asked Clarry.

"Worse. I've never seen anything like it," said Rupe, and he shook his head so that Peter once more had to bite his lip not to smile.

After that the drive was much better, until toward the end, when Rupe happened to mention school. That autumn Peter, who so far only went to day school, was supposed to be joining Rupe at his boarding school.

"You won't be able to escape it this time!" said Rupe cheerfully. "You can't jump off a train twice!"

"Peter did not jump off that train to get out of school!" said Clarry. "He just jumped off because he wanted to. To see if he could."

"Oh did he?" asked Rupe.

"Yes. For fun!"

"Ah."

"Don't say 'ah' like that! You're not so grown-up yet! You did jump off for fun, didn't you, Peter?"

Peter said nothing.

"Didn't you, Peter?"

"Didn't you, Peter?"

"Didn't you, Peter?"

"No I didn't!"

"Peter!" cried Clarry, and knelt up on the seat and beat on her brother's back. Peter swiped backward and Rupe said, "Stop it, kids!"

"And you stop calling us *kids*!" snapped Clarry, and turned her fists on him so hard that Lucy felt the blows through the reins and skipped sideways with her ears flickering.

"Steady Lucy, steady Lucy, steady Luce, good girl," Rupe called to her, as well as he could whilst laughing so much. "Don't upset poor old Lucy, Clarry!"

"Stop calling people kids, then!" said Clarry. "And you made that up about the train, Peter. I know you did. Anyway, Rupe will look after you at school."

Peter flinched, and Rupe noticed and took pity.

"That time we nearly drowned her teaching her to swim," he said to Peter. "Were we right or wrong to fish her out?"

The sounds were a few sleepy midday birds, the rattle of hay cutting in a nearby field, the silky swish of the new rubber tires of the pony trap on the dusty road, and Lucy's hooves, lighter than a *clip-clop*, more of a *trip, trip, trip*.

"I suppose we were right," said Peter at last.

"Nearly there," said Clarry happily. "I'm so hungry. Miss Vane, you know Miss Vane from Sunday School who lives across the road, she made us sandwiches but they were egg and Peter couldn't bear the smell of them. So we dropped them out the window for the seagulls when the line went next to the sea."

"Poor Miss Vane!"

"I know. But egg. She didn't ask, she just made them. Like she did this dress."

Clarry looked down at her dress, which was green and brown check and very bunchy round the middle.

"You should have dropped that out of the window too," said Rupe.

"I've got two other ones so it doesn't matter that it's so horrible. A blue one, and a whitish. The whitish for Sundays. It used to be bright, proper white. Oh Rupe! Peter and me've brought some lovely things. Wait till you see! Some fossils from Yorkshire. A little case of butterflies that our next-door neighbor was throwing away. He was just about to put them on his bonfire, he said! And a frog skeleton, all jumbled up. We're going to make it back into a frog shape again, but we waited for you so you could share. I haven't done proper labels for anything yet; I was saving it for here . . ."

"Oh!" said Rupe like he had suddenly understood something. "For that museum you made!"

"*We* made!" corrected Clarry. "We! All of us!"

"That's right, I helped, didn't I? I'd forgotten all about it."

"You'd forgotten!" repeated Clarry, shocked.

"I've been doing other things."

"I've been doing other things," said Clarry severely, "but I haven't forgotten the museum! And neither has Peter!"

"Shut up, Clarry!" snapped Peter.

"For weeks and weeks it's been the only thing he . . ."

"God!" exploded Peter, which made Rupe grin and Clarry wail, "Why has everything changed? What's the matter with everyone? Aren't we doing the museum this year?"

"*No!*" snarled Peter.

"Yes," said Rupe.

"All of us? You too?"

"Unless Pete's had enough of it."

"Of course he hasn't."

"Well then."

Chapter Four

Morning came in the new bare house. Binny woke, wondered, blinked a bit, and turned comfortably over as she remembered. She had made a wish, the roof had blown off, and she had been delivered to a new world. She pulled back the curtain to inspect it, and found it was all leaves and sky. It looked chilly, and her bed was very warm. She let the curtain fall again, and burrowed back into her pillow.

"Binny, what are you doing?" demanded Clem, arriving in her doorway ten minutes later, all harassed and groomed, as if it was any other weekday. *"Up! Up! Up!"*

"Has something happened? What's the rush?"

Words floated up from the kitchen. Her mother's voice.

"School, of course!"

"School!" exploded Binny, outraged in her pajamas at the top of the stairs.

"SCHOOL NOW THE ROOF'S BLOWN OFF OUR HOUSE!"

"Yes, what else did you think?" Her mother appeared briefly in the hall below to reply. "I'll drive you all in together and then go on to work. And don't start, Binny!"

However Binny, well known for starting, was already well on her way.

"But we only missed one day! I thought we were going to miss weeks and weeks! What about teaching myself with library books? What about looking for Gertie? What do I need to know *anyway* that I don't know already?"

Binny's mother ran her hands through her hair so that it stood up in spikes as she protested, "Binny, not now!" and disappeared again before Binny had even half finished begging, "Can't we even just talk about it?"

"I don't *believe* it!" complained Binny, back in her room, scrambling through the boxes they had packed so hurriedly the day before. There was her uniform. Horrible stuff! Why hadn't she the sense to leave it behind? Binny washed minimally, dragged on her clothes, and stamped down the stairs to find Clem in charge of the kitchen and super efficient.

"Toast," said Clem, handing her a plate.

"No thank you," said Binny.

"Eat and shut up!"

"Sorry, Clem."

"And don't be humble! I've enough to worry about without you being humble!"

Binny drooped before her sister. Clem had everything. Beauty, brains, and a perfect boyfriend, at present away. In another life, in another world, Binny wouldn't have minded him for herself. Half jealous, half sympathetic, she asked Clem, "Are you worried because Liam's at university?"

"Liam?" asked Clem, sounding surprised. "Liam? He's not a problem. As long as he doesn't come home till the end of term I won't have to think about him for weeks."

"Well, I don't see what else you've got to worry about."

Clem, who had been cutting carrot sticks for James's lunch box, put down her knife and took a deep breath, counted to ten, and breathed out again, once more serene. "Pass me an apple for James's lunch!" she said to Binny. "Ham roll, carrot sticks, cheese cubes, ginger cookies, apple, that'll have to do. Look at my hair! All ends!"

"Ends! What ends?" Binny looked with envy at the silky silvery gold on the top of her sister's head. Her own hair was terrible stuff. It broke combs, scattered clips, and tangled around buttons. Once they had cut it short, which led to the discovery of vertical tufts and unmatching ears. "Imagine if you had mine!" she said.

"You could always brush it," said Clem unsympathetically. "Hello James!"

"Hello, don't kiss me," said James, appearing in the doorway with his mother behind him. "Is that my lunch? Can I look?"

"Nope. What are you having for breakfast?"

"Pancakes, with my two eggs from yesterday, and Binny can have some too because of in the night."

Binny blushed with gratitude.

"What happened in the night?" asked his mother.

"He cried," said Binny.

"Nobody heard and nobody heard and nobody heard," said James, "and then Binny came in. Pancakes with golden syrup and orange slices."

"I suppose I've got five minutes," said his mother, flinging flour into a mixing bowl, eggs into the flour, milk into the eggs, and heating a frying pan. "We do have golden syrup; I brought everything out of the kitchen cupboard. Knife!" She sliced an orange while the first pancake cooked, flipped it, passed it to James, and began a second for Binny.

Pancakes restored James. He ate three, and somehow, during the third, his sadness changed to indignation. Gertie was lost and he wanted her back. Or as much of her as possible.

"She can't have just vanished," he said in the car on the way to school. "Even if she got eaten there'd be bits. Legs," he added ruthlessly. "Nothing could ever eat Gertie's scaly old legs!"

"James!"

"Or her beak. Or," he added as they passed a squashed squirrel on the side of the road, "her horrible inside bits. Or . . ."

"Here we are!" said his mother extremely briskly, pulling up outside his school. "Everyone out! Clem and Binny, you can walk from here, can't you? And this afternoon either come home with me, or catch the bus. Come on Binny! Courage! Courage! It can't possibly be that bad!"

Binny climbed out of the car. On the pavement she wavered as if hit by a sudden strong wind, recovered, and walked bravely toward the seething landscape of school.

It really did take courage to push her way through the turmoil in the entrance hall, locate the small grubby locker they had given her on her first day, retrieve the timetable she had hoped never to see again, and to begin the journey to her classroom.

"Oh, it's you!" said Clare as she walked through the door. "Ella, look! She's come back!"

"God," said Ella unenthusiastically.

Binny forgot all Clem's peacemaking advice. "I don't see why it bothers you," she said defensively.

"Because," said Ella, opening a plastic lunch box as she spoke and fishing out a large floppy sandwich, "we have to put up with you, don't we? Live in the same place. Breathe the same air . . ." She took an enormous bite, scattering grated cheese as she chewed.

"Ella!" protested Clare.

"What? I'm hungry!" Ella wedged the rest of her sandwich in her mouth all in one go, and added, grinning, "Actually!"

"Oh shut up!" growled Binny.

Ella snorted with laughter, spraying more cheese. "I bet you were bunking off yesterday, actually, weren't you, actually?"

"No I wasn't!" snapped Binny. "The roof of my house blew off *actually* and we had to move house *actually*. And we've ended up in a freezing cold hole in the middle of nowhere that belongs to some bossy old witchy woman *actually*. And she obviously hates us and the only good part was *actually* that I thought I'd never have to come to this rotten stinking school again! But I had to anyway. So there! *Actually!*"

This speech had a very surprising effect on Clare. She

stopped paying attention to Ella and turned to Binny, staring.

"What?" demanded Binny.

Clare ignored her. "Do you remember?" she said to Ella. "I told you, last night?"

"About Them?" asked Ella, raising her eyebrows.

Clare nodded.

"She's Them?" asked Ella, sounding very shocked indeed. "Did you hear what she just said? Bossy old witchy woman! Freezing cold hole!"

"I know!"

"What's the matter with her?"

Binny did not hear Clare's reply, because she and Ella had turned away, their heads together, their backs so stiff and alien that she dared not go after them. Ella's voice carried back to her, though, as they marched out of the door.

"Mad. I *love* her! Everyone does!"

Following this, a hideous day began.

Everything Binny looked away from for a moment, books, sweater, timetable, vanished to reappear, kicked and grubby, in some distant corner of the floor. Doors swung shut as she was about to walk through them. Shoulders and elbows shoved from behind. Something touched her head and she reached up and found a clot of still warm chewing gum pushed into her hair. Also, anyone who innocently turned her way to speak or smile was stopped immediately with either a flurry of whispers from Ella or an icy glance from Clare.

Binny was shocked by the silent force so suddenly against her. It buffeted and bewildered her until she began to rage.

"You're all *vile*!" she cried, on discovering that someone had wedged a half chewed candy in the keyhole of her locker.

Impassive faces looked away.

"It's not fair!" Binny attempted to wipe her sticky hands on a crumple of tissue. It shredded into rags that fell to the floor. As she scrambled to retrieve them she heard a crunch and there was her pencil case with a dusty footprint on it.

"Everything in that was new!" she shouted. "Everything!"

"New?" asked a silky contemptuous voice.

"What a pity," said another.

"I hate you!" shouted Binny, gathering the remains of her possessions and starting toward the door. "I hate you ALL!" She slammed it open, and there was a teacher on the opposite side.

"It's Binny, isn't it?" asked the slammed-into teacher. "Binny Cornwallis?"

"Belinda, actually," said Clare from behind. Her voice was perfectly normal; friendly even, but at the sound of it Binny swung round.

"You shut up! You just shut up!"

"I'm sorry," said Clare.

"You are *not* sorry!"

"I am, actually."

Right in front of the teacher, Binny hurled her pencil case of broken pencils at Clare's sleek, dark head. A moment later she found herself being very firmly led down the corridor.

The strangest feeling began to wash over Binny. Once at home they had had a door stopper, a fabric cat, stiff and weighted with sand. Now Binny felt like that cat. Immobile. Impossibly heavy. Vaguely she realized that she was actually leaning against a wall.

"Don't you feel well?"

It was the teacher, kind, with her hand on Binny's shoulder.

"Would you like to sit down?"

With a great effort Binny raised her head and moved again.

They took her to a chilly white place called Resources. They asked if she had eaten breakfast and she remembered

Clem's coffee and the pancakes. It was like remembering a scene from a book.

"I'm fine," she told them at last.

Eventually they gave her a pink laminated card, which meant if she showed it to any member of staff she would be allowed to leave the room. Then she was released.

The day became a dreary nightmare with Binny trapped endlessly in its darkness. Students avoided her. Teachers asked how she was. "I'm fine," repeated Binny.

A bell rang; bells had been ringing all day, but this time the people around Binny did not simply swirl and resettle again as if hardly disturbed. This time a new energy lifted and and swept them to the doors. Binny was blown along with them, and all at once, like a sudden awakening, she found herself blinking in clear September sunlight.

Dozens of people from school were streaming toward the bus station. Binny moved with them and then astonishingly, there was Clem. "Brilliant! You're here!"

"Oh, Clem!"

"I thought I'd come and look for you! That's our bus! Come on! Okay?"

Binny nodded. The relief of finding Clem! Of a seat beside the window with her sister between herself and the world! She leaned her face against the cool glass, and felt the rumble of the engine change as the bus moved off. The numbness of the day began to fade. They were passing the place where the airy bubble of a butterfly's world had blown across her own, and she craned to look out of the window. Perhaps, miraculously, it would be there again. It seemed to Binny that if it was, then everything would be all right. The sensible part of her mind knew this could not be true, but another (hopeful, stubborn, ridiculous) part believed in many things that could not possibly be real.

There was no butterfly, and to Binny's horror she found two tears of disappointment trickling down her nose. Hastily she blotted them with her sleeve. Clem was kindly silent.

The bus dropped them at the end of the road to the house.

"I hate school," said Binny as they walked. "That's all."

"Well," said Clem, and then after a minute or two, "if that's all."

Clem, Binny thought, kept all her loves and hates tucked carefully out of the weather.

They found that their mother and James were home before them. James was outside, heaving rocks from the tumbled garden wall and piling them around the hen coop.

"It looks like a Stone Age henhouse," observed Clem.

"I know," agreed James smugly. "I've rocked it all around with just a little gap for the door. Whatever got Gertie'll never climb over that!"

"She might just be lost, not got," said Binny.

"Got," said James cheerfully. "Got and eaten! Don't forget you said you'd look for her, Bin! Legs and things . . ." (Clem moaned and went inside.) "Then we can have a funeral. We haven't had a funeral for ages!"

How nice to be James, thought Binny. What an easy life he lived. No complications. No battering despair. Even a night of loss and tragedy could be redeemed by the happy thought of a funeral. With relief she abandoned her own complicated world and slipped into his.

"Wait till I get these school clothes off and I'll come and help," she said, but by the time she was in her jeans James had stopped building and was suddenly very busy on his bedroom floor with coloring pencils and paper.

"Not homework again!" Binny complained.

"I got another star sticker for my pirate picture," said James. "Get ten stickers and you get a certificate!"

"Then what?"

"What d'you mean, 'then what'? A certificate! With your name on! Wouldn't you want a certificate with your name on?"

"No," said Binny. "I thought we were building Pecker's wall and hunting for Gertie. Come on!"

"I'm doing this now." James rolled aside so that Binny could see, and she bent to peer at the small yellowed rectangle of cardboard he was coloring.

"You didn't draw that!" she said, after one glance.

"I found it," said James. "Can you see what it is?"

"It's a skull. With a beak."

"Yes. Gertie."

"Oh James! That's awful! And we don't know yet that she's dead. Let's go and look for her now, while it's still sunny."

"Couldn't you go without me?"

"No."

"My teacher said probably a fox," said James, sighing but heaving himself to his feet, "but I still think jagular and Dill, you know Dill who sits at my table?"

"How'm I supposed to know Dill who sits at your table?"

"Because . . . !

He sits . . . !

At my table!"

"Oh, all right."

"Dill said, *'Whew!'* Just like that! *'Whew!'* About jagulars. They get you by the throat, Dill said. Do you think it hurts?"

"Not a bit," said Binny untruthfully. They were outside now, and she looked around, considering the landscape of this new home. The garden was just a bit of field enclosed by walls. It sloped away from the house; a slope that got steeper and steeper as it headed downward. There the line of an old railway ran out toward the moors and then on to the old haunted tin mines of the coast.

"I think it would hurt if a jagular got you by the throat," said James. "I don't see how it couldn't. I think it would hurt if *anything* got you by the throat!"

"Nothing is going to get you by the throat," said Binny. "Come on! Down to the old rail line."

"What if there's a train?"

"There hasn't been a train for a hundred years. They don't come farther than the town anymore."

The wild was reclaiming the old line. Its tunnels had become caves from which bats poured at sunset. Wild creatures watched from beneath the blackthorn bushes. Owls waited in the ash trees. In summer lizards basked on the small deserted platforms, in winter deer from the moors came down to its shelter. It was a great place for birds and blackberries and butterflies. Also midges, nettles, and the deep earthy smells of secrets.

"We might be the first people here for years," Binny

told James as they followed the zigzag track down the steep bank.

"What made this path, then?" asked James.

"Animals of course."

James went more slowly.

"Don't you like it here?"

"Do you?" asked James.

"I love it! Oh!"

They both saw it at the same time. A feather, tattered rusty orange, caught in the grasses.

"James?" asked Binny. "Gertie? Is it?"

James nodded. "Yes."

He stooped to pick it up and Binny watched in silence as he stood with his head bent, smoothing the ragged edges back into a feather shape. Briefly he held its curve against his cheek. "Gertie," he murmured, and suddenly turned and began scrambling very quickly back up the way they had come.

"James!" protested Binny.

"I've got to do my homework."

"But it's just getting exciting!"

"I don't want it to be exciting," said James, not pausing in his hurry.

"Wait just one minute. I can see more orange." Binny

hurried on a few steps farther, and this time there was a whole bunch of feathers, still in the fan shape in which they had been dropped. "Lots more," she called up to James. "A whole handful!"

"A mouthful," said James. "I'm going back to the house."

"Oh James, don't be silly! This is the best place we've found for ages and ages!"

But James would not listen. He disappeared up the last of the slope and vanished completely.

Binny did not follow. She could not understand James. The overgrown valley seemed a friendly place to her. In the world above, autumn had arrived, but this place was so sheltered that here summer still remained. Brown and orange butterflies lifted from blackberry bushes as she passed. A patch of late harebells made a puddle of fallen sky.

At the bottom of the zigzag track the ground was more open. A line of wooden sleepers from the old railway made a path that was comfortable to follow. Binny wandered along it until she found a patch of sun-dried grass and small yellow flowers. There she flopped down, and soon, in ones and twos, small movements began all around her.

Rabbits.

Binny knew nothing of the countryside. Except for the

last few weeks, she had lived all her life on city streets. The rabbits were an astonishment to her. Their numbers. Their rocking-horse hops and sudden quivering pauses. The cheerful bounce of their white flag tails. She forgot about Gertie, and the horrible day at school, and watched, enchanted. How lucky that just when she needed it, she had found a private world.

An hour passed. The sun disappeared. The shadows became blue, and then gray. A voice called from high above, *Binny, Binny, Binny!* Binny stood, scattering rabbits, and began to hurry back, along the track and up the slope, across the tumbled wall and the shabby garden, until she stood blinking in the brightness of the large bare kitchen.

"Oh!" exclaimed Clem, seeing the handful of feathers. "Poor Gertie!"

"And poor Pecker," said James, taking the feathers. "Now she's got to lay eggs all on her own!"

"As soon as we are home again we'll get a new friend for Pecker," promised the children's mother, busy as usual, stirring pasta sauce, pairing socks, and filling in a new address form for James's school, "unless . . ."

"Unless Pecker gets grabbed as well," said James, reaching for the cookie tin, "but she won't because of my stones."

"James! You're dropping crumbs all over the floor," said his mother. "Find a plate!"

James fetched a plate and began arranging Gertie's orange feathers on it. He made a feather Gertie with a cookie head.

"For dinner," he said, presenting this very suddenly under Binny's nose, "it is chicken!"

"I thought you were sad about Gertie," exclaimed Binny.

"I am. That's why I'm being so careful about her poor dead feathers."

"Wash your hands James, if you want any supper," his mother told him. "And don't eat that cookie you've been playing with."

"Why not?"

"It will be all germy."

"Why will it?"

"Because feathers are all germy."

"But if Gertie is dead, won't her germs be dead?"

"No they won't."

"Well that's not fair."

"James! Hands!"

James washed his hands but he still did not get any supper because just at that moment there was a loud thumping on the door and it was the woman from the night before, the owner of the house.

"I came with the bus timetable, which I thought might be useful, and I have to say I'm not pleased," she began, the moment the door was opened. "I see you've been taking stone from the wall and I'm going to have to ask you to stop. And don't try putting it back again yourself because that's a specialist job. I don't know," she added, although she did not say what she did not know.

"I am so, so sorry," said the children's mother earnestly. "I'm afraid James . . ." She looked around for James, but he had vanished. ". . . really wouldn't have realized. But I should have. And thank you very much for thinking of us with the timetable."

"We *try* to look after our guests," said the woman indignantly, "and we *hope* that in return . . . Well, I'll say no more. Good night."

"Good night, I am sorry, you must think . . ."

But the woman had turned away.

"It's my fault," said the children's always-brave mother. "I should have thought. I should have watched James. I should have had that roof checked at the beginning of summer . . ." And then, to Binny's utter astonishment, she turned her face toward the kitchen door and leaned there, her head on her arm.

It was only for a moment; by the time Binny's alarmed

eyes had found Clem's, it was over as if it had never been.

"Supper!" she said, smiling at Binny. "Pasta. Ice cream. Shout James, someone. How useful to have a bus time-table. Binny, could you put some knives and forks and things out? Aren't we going to miss this lovely big kitchen when we get home, Binny, Bin, Belinda, Bel?"

Binny nodded, the evening resumed, but because of that small moment by the kitchen door she made up her mind not to worry her mother with one word about school. Not then, or ever, no matter how bad it became.

Summer 1913, Part 2

That summer the museum was different. Rupe helped as much as ever, but in a slightly amused, grown-out-of-it kind of way. Peter worked passionately, traveling miles on his bike to scour new locations. Once again, the museum moved house, back to its starting place in the large bare room where Peter slept. It became very organized. In the quest for perfection several less perfect items, including the mole, were evicted. Soon Peter's camp bed followed.

"You can't sleep on the landing!" Clarry objected. "Everyone falls over you!"

"Who cares?" asked Peter, although after a few days of being fallen over he grew tired of it himself, and installed his bed in the bathroom that he shared with Clarry and Rupe.

In this inconvenient place he stayed. Clarry and Rupe put up with it, because it was the summer when everyone was putting up with Peter. Nobody wanted another drastic, school-avoiding accident. Peter would not discuss school, except to say what he had been saying ever since he was seven and first heard of the hideous place: "If you make me go there I will die." It was no good anyone pointing out that Rupe went there, and far from dying, had become excellent at a dozen sports, made a hundred friends, learned a thousand jokes, and lived in fear of nothing, not even falling off the chapel roof, which he regularly climbed.

"I'm not Rupe," Peter would say, and his face would become tight and pale so that the bones of his skull showed through the skin. Then his family would shut up. They knew Peter was clever. If he could be got through the summer without accident he would go to school and settle down. There was every chance that after that he would earn a scholarship for university and be well on the way to living happily ever after as a mad professor. There would be no limit then to the museums he might set up.

But first he had to go to school.

Chapter Five

At school things were becoming worse and worse. Every day Binny marched in, so defensive and grumpy that even non-enemies avoided her. Clare made remarks: "It's actually stopped raining." Ella exploded with giggles. Somehow the timetable in the front of her homework diary was rewritten with all the wrong rooms. She learned to check chairs for superglue before she sat down.

For a day or two, Binny tried fighting back; she could slam doors just as hard as Clare and Ella, and if Clare could say "Actually" she could say "Mummy."

"How's Mummy?" she asked Clare, and Clare's eyes widened with fury and Binny was pleased.

And then she did something that was too bad.

She did it to Ella's lunch box. Ella, despite her size, wore ballet shoes to school. Their soles were worn and slippery; Ella slithered on tiled washroom floors, and skidded when it rained. One wet morning, in an effort to cross the entrance hall quickly enough to shove Binny against a door, she lost her balance.

"Ha!" said Binny, doing a bit of shoving of her own.

Ella stumbled, papers fell, books fanned open on the damp hall floor, and her lunch box appeared at Binny's feet.

Binny and her possessions had endured a lot from Ella. The lunch box was a gift. She gave it a good hard kick.

Tomatoes, cookies, cheese slices, and half a pork pie were scattered across the hall. Ella chased after them in her uncertain shoes. People sniggered, and not, for once, at Binny. Ella did not seem to notice. Everything she managed to grab she ate, as if to keep it safe.

Binny stood against a wall and watched and felt quite numb and uninvolved, and while that feeling lasted she was all right. But it faded very quickly, and then all morning she was tormented. Why had she not picked the lunch box up and handed it back to Ella? How would the story have gone then? She flinched from the thought of Ella's frantic gathering.

If Clem had seen, or James, or her mother.

If Gareth had seen, or Max.

If her father . . .

At lunchtime Binny took out her lunch money and placed it on the table in front of Ella.

"You'd better have that," she said, and walked away.

That was the worst day, and she didn't try fighting again.

Binny had no friends. It had never happened to her before. In her other schools there had always been a group, bickering sometimes, telling secrets, going off in huffs now and then, but always coming together to listen to each other's stories, weave complicated plans, pounce on each other to exclaim, *You'll never guess!* Now there was no one. At home Binny said nothing, not even to Clem; she was ashamed to have no friends. However, one Saturday morning, out of loneliness, she told Gareth.

Gareth was not very sympathetic, but at least he understood.

"I worked it out ages ago when everyone at school was after me," he told Binny, "and in the end I decided I wasn't that bothered because for one thing, they were all really stupid (compared to me) . . ."

"Yes but . . ."

"And for another, it's not surprising if nobody likes you because most people don't like most people. It's statistics!"

"What?" said Binny.

"Say, everyone in the world likes about ten people," said Gareth. "And there's about seven and a half billion people in the world. What's the chance of ever meeting anyone you like? Or anyone who likes you?"

There was something wrong with Gareth's logic that Binny could not quite name. Perhaps the ten people?

"Only ten people?" she asked.

"I think that's about right," said Gareth calmly. "There's four people I actually like in the world, and six I quite like. (There used to be seven, but I knocked one off.) And that includes my family, as well as three dogs . . . What's the matter? Stop it! Stop laughing!"

But for a minute the combination of relief at having told someone and Gareth's cold-blooded statistics were too much for Binny and she could not stop laughing.

"I don't see what's so funny," said Gareth, who seldom did see what was so funny. "Are you just obsessed with school, or has anything else been happening?"

Binny told Gareth about the new bare house, the disappearance of Gertie, and the discovery of the old railway line with its rabbits and green shadows and possibility of foxes.

Gareth became much more human at the mention of foxes.

"If you see anything like that," he said, "a fox or a badger or anything, don't go telling people."

"Why not?"

"Secret is safe. Lots of people don't like them. They'd get rid of them if they could. So if you see them, keep it quiet. Just in case."

"What, not even tell you?"

"Well, of course tell me!" said Gareth, sounding so shocked that Binny laughed again, and two hundred and sixty miles away Max heard her and barked in response.

"Is Max one of the four people that you really like?" asked Binny.

"'Course he is," said Gareth. "Max, David Attenborough, someone who used to walk their alsatian where I take Max but I haven't seen them for ages, you!"

Binny was suddenly giddy with happiness. To be one of the four! Right at the top, with Max and David Attenborough and the unknown vanished dog-walker. To be liked by one of the most antisocial people in the world! At the end of the conversation she put the phone down feeling better than she had for ages. Outdoors was a perfect autumn day, a cool blue sky and thick damp grass scattered with September leaves. Inside Binny could hear a vacuum cleaner humming, Clem's hair dryer as she got ready to leave for her Saturday job at the café in town, and a sudden urgent knocking at her bedroom door. She opened it to find James with his arms full of cardboard and straw.

"Can I put this in your room?" he demanded.

"No you can't!"

"Just for a little while."

"Why?"

"I've got to tidy mine."

Tidy bedrooms had been ordered that morning because once again the woman who owned the house was about to visit. This time she had left a message to say that she would be along to look at the windows. The news had left the children's mother baffled, but firm. Clem's room was always tidy, Binny had managed by stuffing everything into her giant-sized wardrobe and locking the door, but James's was a terrible mess. After Binny had found the orange feathers he had begun making a luxury chicken coffin with Sellotape and cardboard and straw. He was always taking it apart to add extra treats, such as plasticine eggs, chicken food, and windows. He had done this so often that the Sellotape lost its stickiness, the sides became loose, and the straw and chicken food and other things fell out. Binny looked at the trail of coffin bits leading up to her bedroom door and said, "Take it outside and bury it."

"Not yet. I've only got those few feathers. There might be more things we still haven't found."

"I couldn't see any."

"You only looked once. Can I just leave this in your room until she's gone?"

"No of course you can't. Shove it under your bed or something. When's she coming?"

"She's in the kitchen *now*."

"Now!" exclaimed Binny, and grabbed her jacket and skittered down the stairs to the front door.

"Where are you going?"

"Out! To look for more feathers!" called Binny, and she was gone.

The old railway was different that morning. Right from the first moments, Binny knew. The grit rolled under her sneakers as she skidded down the path, just as it had before. There were still brown butterflies on the bramble flowers and the flicker of rabbits in the corners of her vision. The air had the same earthy sweetness. Outwardly, it had not changed, but a week of being hunted at school had made Binny very wary.

There was a feeling of tension everywhere.

Binny remembered Gareth's badgers and foxes. She trod very carefully and she paused often to look around. Once, amongst the bushes, she thought she saw a gentle movement, as if a shadow had turned. For a long time she stood waiting, although for what she did not know. A glimpse of russet? A stripy face? Dark eyes under branching antlers?

Nothing.

After a while she went on again, and then, in the soft mud beside a deep puddle, she found footprints. Lots of prints. There were light hesitant marks, larger than a mouse, smaller than a rabbit, blurry and pricked with tiny claws. Also quite clearly a paw print, definitely a paw; she could see the shape of the pads.

And, over all the others, massive, four-toed stampings, like the prints of a giant chicken. Binny looked, and looked again. Could they be Gertie, still alive? Were Gertie's feet that big? Were any chicken's? These prints were enormous. Prehistoric. Huge bird prints, that made pictures in her mind of ostriches and eagles and dinosaurs with wings.

I wish Gareth could see them, thought Binny, as she bent closer to look.

"HEY!"

The whole of Binny jumped and froze at the frightened, frightening cry.

"YOU!"

Binny's heart banged in panic.

"YOU! HEY YOU!"

She spun round and round, searching for the source of the voice.

"CLEAR OFF!"

Oh! thought Binny, and she stared in surprise and dismay.

Small, against the dark mouth of an abandoned tunnel. Trembling with temper. Outraged. Glaring.

"GO AWAY. AND STAY AWAY!

OR ELSE!"

It was Clare shouting. Clare standing in the mouth of the tunnel, attacking with threats. "GO AWAY AND STAY AWAY OR ELSE!"

"OR ELSE WHAT?" demanded Binny, so Clare tried another attack.

"GROCKLE GIRL!"

Binny must have blinked, and in that second Clare was gone, but laughter echoed from the tunnel.

For a moment or two Binny stood, stunned. Tormented in school, and now tormented at home.

"GROCKLE GIRL! GROCKLE GIRL! GROCKLE GIRL!" called the echoes.

All at once, Binny exploded into movement. She fixed her eyes on the place where Clare had been and ran, leaping the bramble trip wires spreading across her way, pushing past the rough fencing that had once guarded the entrance to the tunnel, following a narrow path of trodden earth and gravel, charging toward the echoes.

The light in the tunnel grew dim very quickly, and

Binny was forced to slow down. That was when she began to hear the noises all around. The sound of her own footsteps. A faint and high-pitched staccato of alarmed, invaded bats. The plink of water dripping into water. A breath of unfriendly laughter.

Deeper and deeper. The track became a rubble of large, loose stones, laced with ancient rubbish. The ground was damp, and then wet, and then slippery and puddled. The air smelled of soot and ammonia, sulfur and dirt and oily decay. The way curved and became utterly black.

Binny stumbled and fell very hard in the dark.

Plink-plink-plink went the water that oozed from the roof, but now, apart from Binny's gasping breaths, there was no other sound at all. No one moved when she moaned, "Oh" and and rocked with the pain. No one sniggered as she sniffed a bit and got to her feet.

"Help!" said Binny, not loudly, but loud enough for someone helpful to hear. "Please help!" she said, much louder, groping round and round in the dark. Anyone, helpful or unhelpful, could have heard that time.

Plink! went the water, but there was no other sound.

It was a long way back to the light.

To Binny, stiff kneed, sore handed, plastered with mud, guided only by the touch of the slippery walls, it seemed to take hours. Only very gradually did the darkness become less black. After a while she discovered small arched hollows in the tunnel walls. Then she understood. Clare must have stood and waited in one of these, while she, Binny, continued into the dark.

At last the light grew brighter. She got along faster then, and presently stood at the entrance again, half dazed and staring about.

The old railway line was alive with noise. Wood pigeons clattered. A blackbird scolded. A flock of sparrows erupted from the bushes to Binny's left.

"HEY!" shouted Binny, and a great silence fell. No birds. No answering laughter. No footsteps. No snap of twigs, nor rustle of leaves, nor breath of wind.

But, very close, a sigh.

Huff.

And on the edge of unseen, a slow amber blink.

The same careful movement of shadow in the low bushes on the left.

A pause in time.

Then the sounds came back. A small plane droning overhead, the rustle of wings in the bushes, and traffic far away.

Binny was back in the everyday world again. She checked the damage from her fall and found that her head was throbbing and that while she had been standing her knees had tightened into two stiff lumps of pain. She touched the bump in her hair, and her sore hand came away sticky with blood.

Blood was impressive, but also slightly alarming. Binny decided she had better get home.

It was hard to get going, a slow climb up the zigzag path, a heavy trudge across the rough grass of the garden to the kitchen door. Only James was in the room. "Hello, don't kiss me, I'm very busy," he said from under the kitchen table.

"Where's Mum?"

"Upstairs."

"What are you doing?"

"It's a surprise. Go away."

"I've cut my hands."

"Bleeding?" asked James, who did not like blood.

"Yes."

"Yuck," said James.

Binny looked at her stinging hands. She looked at her knees and was not surprised to see dark patches of blood oozing through the denim of her jeans. She tried to pull off her sneakers but their laces were in such mud soaked knots that her sore fingers could not manage them. Get clean, she thought. Find some fresh clothes.

Very slowly she began to climb the stairs.

And there in her bedroom was Clare.

Binny stood in the doorway, battered, bloody, patched, and splashed from head to feet with mud and slime, smelling of earth and drains and ooze, and shivering a little. Everyone in the room was staring at her, her mother, the woman who owned the house, and Clare.

Clare was smiling in delight.

The woman who owned the house was the first to speak.

"What have you done?" she asked. "Belinda! It's Belinda, isn't it?"

"Binny actually," murmured Clare.

This was too much for Binny. "You!" she erupted. "You! What are you doing here?"

"Binny, stop!" ordered her mother, suddenly with her. "Are you hurt? Show me your hands! How have you managed to get into such a state?"

"Why is she here?"

"Clare? Clare? What on earth is the matter with you Binny? Clare has done nothing but very kindly help her mother measure for winter curtains! Why shouldn't she be here? And where have you been?"

Binny took a great indignant breath and then stopped. If she said where she'd been she knew quite well what would happen. She'd be ordered never to go there again. She stared at her mother, speechless, trying to think, and just in time, James saved her.

He appeared behind her at the top of the stairs, all glowing with pride. "I've got the back off that big television that didn't work properly!" he announced. "I found a box of screwdrivers in that cupboard they think we can't unlock and I . . . Oh!"

He screwed shut his eyes. He opened them again. He looked at Clare and her mother and pushed out his bottom lip. "I thought they'd gone," he said.

So Binny was able to slink away to the bathroom and to peel off her muddy clothes, and dab her sore hands and knees and get used to the idea that the house in which she was living was owned by Clare's family.

It was Clare's family who lived just up the road.

It was Clare's mother who came so often to check on them.

Then Binny remembered, with anguish, her words at school to Clare and Ella. *And we've ended up in a freezing cold hole in the middle of nowhere that belongs to some bossy old witchy woman.*

"*Oh!*" wailed Binny, so loudly that her mother heard and abandoned James to rush in demanding, "Now what?"

"Everything. Nothing. It doesn't matter. The soap hurts my cuts."

"They're filthy! Here . . ."

Binny's mother pushed in the bath plug, reached for a bottle of disinfectant, poured a terrible amount into the bath, and turned on both taps.

The air filled with steam and there was a smell like the school toilets on the first day of term. From downstairs came a crash and James's voice, "I was *only* lifting it back!"

"In! Soak! And turn the taps off again!" ordered her mother, and shot back out of the bathroom.

Binny lay in the murky (but germ killing) water and thought, if this was a story, I would tear all the pages out, right back to the day before school. In her mind she did that, edited the fallen-leaf wish (closing school forever), took her foot off the birthday card, unflattened the birthday flowers, unsquashed the birthday cake, and arrived tidily on the pavement beside Clare in time to say, "Look at that butterfly!" and to hear Clare reply, "Oh yes."

It was all very comforting until the bath water went cold, and then things became very uncomfortable indeed.

Summer 1913, Part 3

The museum had changed, more serious, less shared, but Clarry was still the label writer and the museum cards she made were done as carefully as ever:

Late Cretaceous Ammonite

(*Bostrychoceras*)

Filey Beach, Yorkshire

1913

(Found by R. Smith, aged 14. Swapped for the pen Peter had from Clarry on his birthday.)

"I knew you were mad about me swapping that pen," said Peter when he saw the label.

"I wasn't," said Clarry untruthfully.

"It didn't write very well anyway."

"I know. You told me before."

Rarely did it dawn on Peter that other people had feelings as painful as his own, but now it did, and he gave her an awkward sort of pat and said, "Sorry."

"It's all right," said Clarry, immediately forgiving everything he had ever done to her throughout the whole of her life. She hugged him, and was allowed to do it.

The frog was terribly difficult. In the end they laid it out on black cardboard, like a map of a frog, and fixed it into place with tiny dabs of glue from Clarry's finest paintbrush.

Skeleton of Common Frog
(*Rana temporaria*)
Assembled July 1913
from a broken up skeleton bought by Peter
in a junk shop in Plymouth
(Incomplete)

"It looks completely complete to me," remarked Rupe, who had been playing in a tennis tournament in town during the whole of the reconstruction.

"She lost two bones," said Peter grimly. "Dropped them. And we never found them."

"Well, who would know?" asked Rupe. "And who would care? Not even the frog! What's two bones more or less, when you've lost your skin and stuffing?"

Peter began slamming furiously about the room.

"Now what?" Rupe asked him.

"Nothing. I'm going."

"Oh, Peter," exclaimed Clarry. "Rupe was just joking. He didn't mean anything!"

Peter shrugged.

"Where are you going? Can I come too?"

"To the moor. No you can't," said Peter, and banged out of the room before she could reply.

Clarry and Rupe looked helplessly at each other.

"Come on then Clarry," said Rupe. "Tell me what all that was about."

"You laughed at him."

"I didn't. I laughed at his frog."

"He wants it to be perfect."

"The frog? You dropped the blooming bones, not me!"

"No, no. He was nice about the bones after he stopped being cross. He said as long as we said incomplete on the label it would be all right."

"What, then? What's got to be perfect?"

"The museum. This summer. Everything."

Rupe, who had recently taken to raising one eyebrow, now did this.

"Don't make everything a joke!" protested Clarry. "And don't do that!"

"You smiled."

"I didn't."

"Saw you smile! Now shut up, Clarry. Don't talk. I'm having a good idea."

He stood at the window, watching Peter haul his bike from the old building that had held the museum the year before. After a while he grinned very suddenly.

"What?" asked Clarry, who had been watching his face.

"Clarry, you like all this natural history stuff, don't you?"

"Of course I do. Why?"

"Nothing, nothing. Just a thought."

"Something for the museum?"

"Perhaps. Sort of. If I can manage it."

"It's something special for Peter, isn't it?" asked Clarry, glowing.

"All these questions!" said Rupe. "If it's going to happen I've got to go and see someone. Will you be all right on your own?"

"Oh yes! I've something special to do too. It will take me ages."

Clarry's something special was her most careful labeling yet. She spent the day drawing a plan of the butterfly case, with each butterfly in its correct place, outlined in Indian ink. Underneath the outlines, after a lot of anxious hunting in the butterfly book, she printed their names in English and Latin.

"I think they're right. I'm almost sure they are," she said, showing it to Rupe, who was home before Peter.

"It's a work of art!" said Rupe. He was truly surprised. He looked at it again, and then at Clarry, as if she might have somehow changed while he had been gone. She hadn't; she was the same round faced, shabby little Clarry, eyebrows too dark, hair too wild, clothes never quite right, no matter how often her grandmother took her shopping.

Also, as always, she was spilling over with questions.

"Did you see the person you wanted to see? Can you manage what it is you said you might manage? Will you tell me what it is? What else have you been doing?"

"Yes. Perhaps. No. Tennis in the park."

"Oh."

"Pete's been gone ages now."

"I know. Six hours and a bit. Do you think you could check the butterflies if I brought you the book?"

It had taken Clarry most of the six and a bit hours to

Aglais urticae

Callophrys rubi

Erynnis tages

draw and label the butterflies. Rupe checked them in three minutes, saying, "Yep. Yep. Perfect. Ten out of ten!"

"Thirty!" said Clarry. "There are thirty."

"Are there really? Clever old you!" said Rupe.

"The brown ones were hard."

"I bet they were. Hey, Clarry, have you got this right? Skipper? Dingy Skipper? Are you sure there's a butterfly called that?"

"Yes. Definitely. I know Dingy Skipper is right."

"Well, if you say so." Rupe turned over the plan of the butterflies and wrote in curling flourishing letters on the back:

This case of thirty British butterflies was donated to
the collection by Miss Clarry Penrose
(Who also drew the magnificent key!)
July 1913

"Rupe!" exclaimed Clarry. "You shouldn't have put that!"

"Oh yes I should."

"Not magnificent! What will Peter say?"

"Peter will love it."

Clarry looked down at her cramped and inky fingers and hoped he was right. Her hand ached at the thought of doing it all again. Let Peter be pleased, she willed, and it worked and he was.

He was back too late for supper, but so bad tempered with hunger that the entire household rushed to feed him. Clarry sat and watched while he consumed ham and tomatoes, cold potatoes and lettuce salad, an omelette, a pint of milk, and half an apple pie.

"Now do you feel better?" she asked at last.

"There was nothing wrong with me. I was only hungry."

"I made a key for the butterflies while you were out. Shall I show you?"

"I expect you will," said Peter, yawning and lazy for once, from so much food and fresh air.

"There!" said Clarry, triumphantly handing over her masterpiece.

"Hmmm," said Peter, and then, after several tense, wide-awake, scrutinizing minutes, "Clarry. Not bad!"

"Rupe checked it."

"What, properly?" asked Peter. "Rupe? Oh well, it looks all right. Quite good actually! You've got the browns sorted this time. You called a Meadow Brown a Hedge Brown the other day when we were out."

"They move so quickly, before I can tell."

"And the three Fritillaries! Did Rupe help with them?"

"No. He was out doing tennis or something."

"Tennis!" said Peter scornfully. "Anyway, well done! Really not bad. Thanks, Clarry!"

Clarry sparkled with pleasure, but felt compelled to say, "Rupe wrote on the back."

"Oh," said Peter, turning it over. "Well. Magnificent. I suppose . . ."

Peter looked up at Clarry with one of his rare, transforming smiles. "I suppose it is!"

He put it on the table (carefully, Clarry noticed with pleasure), picked up the butterfly book, and became lost. However, half an hour later, when he looked up and found she was still sitting there he rummaged round in his knapsack and held out a small cardboard box.

"Look at this!"

Clarry lifted the lid. Another butterfly, dark wings above, bright jade underneath.

"Hairstreak," said Peter. "Green."

"What a funny name."

"No it isn't."

"Where did you find it?"

"On the moor."

"Dead?"

Peter rolled his eyes.

"It's not as pretty as the Peacocks and Tortoiseshells."

"It's a lot more important than Peacocks and Tortoise-shells!"

"Is it?"

"Rarer."

"I still like the Peacocks best," said Clarry, and then she suddenly remembered. "Rupe's getting something for us! Something really special. He's trying to arrange it. He wouldn't tell me what."

"About time Rupe did something," said Peter, hanging over his butterfly box.

"What do you think it will be? What would be fantastic, Peter?"

Peter was silent for so long that Clarry thought he had forgotten.

"A Purple Hairstreak. A Large Blue. A White Admiral. A Silver Spotted Skipper. A Swallowtail."

They flitted before Clarry's eyes, purple, blue, white, silver.

"What color is a Swallowtail?"

Peter turned to the picture in the book.

"Lemon yellow, edged with black," he said, his voice

husky with the thought. "Some blue. And a bit of red. Not much. See?"

"Like a ruby," said Clarry, hanging over his shoulder.

"A dusty ruby."

"Is a Swallowtail special?"

"Most special of them all."

Chapter Six

When Binny appeared in the kitchen after her bath, clean but damp and smelling like a swimming pool, James pointed secretly at their mother and whispered a warning.

"She's cross," whispered James.

He was right.

"When Mrs. Tremayne has been so kind!"

The children's mother was spectacular in her anger, her voice ice laden, her hair all vertical spikes. "Taking us in at such short notice. Worrying about curtains and bus timetables! Hot water bottles! Wine!"

"I never had none of that wine," said James.

"I was ashamed of you both! Binny! Speaking to Clare like that! And as for you, James . . ."

"It was the sort of TV they had in the olden days. I was fixing it."

"Was that what crashed?" asked Binny.

"Because I was putting it back, it crashed," said James. "Because I wasn't allowed to fix it."

"Half your pocket money for the rest of your life," said his mother. "That's what it will cost you! And you can write to Mrs. Tremayne and apologize!"

"A sorry letter?" asked James, who although only six years old had had a good deal of experience with sorry letters since he learned to write.

"Yes, one of those."

"Can't I just say it?"

"No, you can't just say it. You can write it down properly. But first you are going to clear up your bedroom. What on earth have you got under your bed? No! Don't start telling me! Just go and get rid of it! Now! Go! Shoo! Close the door!"

She waited until his footsteps could be heard on the stairs and said, "Binny."

"I just fell over, that's all."

"You know I'm not talking about that. The way you spoke to Clare in front of her mother! She was *helping*, Binny! Like you and Clem help me. Do you know, before you came in, her mother and I were saying how lucky we were to have girls that helped us out! And then you made that dreadful scene! What on earth was it all about?"

Binny thought of the friendless school, the slammed

doors, shattered pencil case, kicked possessions. The whispers and glances. Clare, standing in the shadows of the tunnel as she, Binny, blundered into the treacherous dark. She thought of those things, but she did not want to explain them to her mother.

"It was because she said '*actually,*'" she said at last. "About my name. '*Binny, actually,*' she said."

"But what's wrong with that?" asked Binny's baffled mother. "She was explaining that your name was usually shortened to Binny."

"It was the way she said it."

"She didn't say it like *anything*! I know. I was there. Well, you can apologize to Clare next time you see her. And this afternoon you can clean the bathroom, which is now knee-deep in mud. And while you're busy you can think hard about whether you want Gareth and Max to visit us at Christmas . . ."

"Mum!"

"Because if you do, we need a new roof. And a new roof quickly costs more than a new roof slowly. So I will have to work extra shifts. Which will mean quite often leaving you and James here with Clem. If I can trust you to behave."

"I don't want you to have to do even more work."

"Binny, that's the least of my problems!"

"What's the most?"

"You wouldn't believe me if I told you!"

Binny, problem child, cleaned the bathroom, the trail of mud up the stairs, and the kitchen floor. She vacuumed James's bedroom carpet. She would have helped him with his letter but he did not want help.

"I've started liking writing sorry letters," he said. "I've done two practice ones and two real ones."

"Why two?"

"Because I was so sorry," said James cheerfully, enveloping his letter very thoroughly with extra Sellotape and drawing on a stamp. "I think that looks good. I bet she's excited. I hope she writes me one back!"

Letter writing, Binny noticed, seemed to have cleared James's conscience of all traces of guilt.

"What are you going to do now?" she asked him.

"Build an avalanche down the stairs," said James, and left the room as lightly and airily as a boy freshly made.

Binny did not follow. The morning still haunted her. She thought of the sharp sunlight and the half seen movements in the shadows. She remembered the urgent anger of Clare's first screech.

I was just looking at the footprints, thought Binny.

★ ★ ★

Once again, she telephoned Gareth.

Gareth ignored all the Clare related stuff ("Don't go on about all that again!") and all the darkness-in-the-tunnel stuff ("What did you expect? Chandeliers?").

"Tell me again about the footprints," he said impatiently.

"Well," said Binny reluctantly, knowing he would snort. "They were so big. Like a giant . . . oh, it doesn't matter."

"Giant what?"

"Chicken."

Gareth snorted.

"I didn't say they were a giant chicken," said Binny with dignity. "I said they were like a giant chicken. What other big birds are there? A swan? An eagle?"

Far away in Oxfordshire, Binny heard Gareth sigh.

"Why not an eagle?"

"Bin, you wouldn't recognize an eagle if it came down and sat on your head. Can you get hold of a mobile phone with a camera?"

"Yes, we've got a shared one now. We got it after you and me got stuck on that rock and nearly drowned."

"Well, go and get it. Find a ruler. Go back to where you saw the prints. Put the ruler by the print. Take a photo. Send it to me. It'll be a heron."

"A *fish*?"

"Her*on*, not her*ring*! Hurry up!"

"But . . ."

"Get on. I'm waiting!"

"My knees!" protested Binny. "They've just been all bandaged!"

"So?"

Gareth had gone, the mobile phone was lying on the kitchen table, Binny went.

HA HA. QUITE GOOD. ALMOST HAD ME.

That was the message Gareth sent in return for his giant chicken footprint. It was so typical that Binny could almost hear his voice. Slightly triumphant. Never-to-be-caught-out.

WHAT DO U MEAN? she demanded in return. U SAID SEND IT. U SAID A HER . . .

Binny paused. Heron or herring? Better be on the safe side.

U SAID U KNEW WHAT IT WAS.

Gareth's next message was equally unhelpful.

I BET YOU CAN'T FIND ANOTHER.

Binny found another giant chicken footprint easily, in seconds.

ARE YOU TRYING TO BE FUNNY? wrote the ungrateful Gareth.

What was the matter with him? complained Binny to herself. Here she was, doing just as he had asked, and was he pleased? No. He was in a mood.

U ARE IN A MOOD, Binny told him, and then waited and waited and waited and waited and nothing arrived.

Clem was in the kitchen when Binny got back to the house. Perhaps Clem noticed the mobile phone, dumped back on the kitchen table. Perhaps she noticed the way Binny checked it, every thirty seconds or so.

"Gareth?" she asked.

"I'm not calling him if he won't call me," said Binny.

"That's the spirit!" said Clem.

Everyone laughed, and it became a normal Saturday again. James posted his sorry letter through the farmhouse letterbox.

"I'd tried to do it secretly," he said, "but when I looked up Clare was watching out of the window of the room right over the door. She laughed."

"She would," said Binny grimly.

Clem went upstairs with her flute. Pecker produced another egg. Binny's mother made soup and Binny learned to make cheese scones. They were golden and perfect and their toasted cheese smell seemed to warm the whole house.

James, for whom the novelty of homework had not yet worn off, bent busily over his newsbook.

My only chkn lade an egg, he wrote. *It had a date on it. Soss pish os.*

"What does that mean?" asked Binny.

"I know what it means," said James. He drew a picture of the egg but it didn't come out well so he added spots, purple and yellow and green.

"Horrible Gareth would say that wasn't scientifically accurate," remarked Binny, still conscious of the silent phone beside her on the table.

"Why is he horrible?" asked James.

"Because he's in a mood," said Binny, and just as she spoke the phone erupted into messages.

WAS THAT FIRST PHOTO FOR REAL?

OR WERE YOU JUST MESSING ABOUT?

FAKING STUFF?

DID YOU JUST TAKE IT?

DID YOU JUST POINT THE CAMERA AT THE GROUND AND TAKE IT?

YES, wrote Binny. OF COURSE. FUSS FUSS FUSS YOU'RE STILL IN A MOOD. CRIKEY.

After this exchange the phone went quiet again.

A surprising thing happened that afternoon. Mrs. Tremayne knocked on the door. "That's for your James," she said to Binny, who happened to be the one to open it, and handed her a bar of chocolate. It was a very small bar, the smallest in fact, that it was possible to buy, but still, chocolate.

"Oh!" said Binny, astonished. "Thank . . ."

"We're all out for the day today. Should you be wanting us we'll be back around eight."

"Mrs. Tremayne," said Binny bravely, "I'm sorry if I was . . ."

"Yes," said Mrs. Tremayne, and left.

"It's because of my letter," said James, when Binny took the chocolate up to his room. "I knew it was good."

"What did it say?"

James held out a worn looking sheet of paper, one of his practice letters, and Binny read:

> I am sory I mendd yor tele tel tv.
> I AM SOry I unlokd the cbod you lokd.
> You lef the keys in a drawr so I did.
> Now I wont any mor.

And the stons of the wall for my chikn Peker

to kepe her safe.

Lots of love from James Cornwallis age 6

xxxooo

o meens hug

"I am sorry I unlocked the cupboard you locked," Binny read out loud. "You left the keys in a drawer . . . James? You've gone bright red!"

"No I haven't."

"You're up to something! What did you do with the keys?"

"Gave them to Mummy."

It was the word *Mummy* that gave him away, more than the suddenly dropped golden head, more than the quickened breathing.

Binny looked at her little brother, face hidden, ears flaming scarlet, left hand clutched tight in his pocket, and asked, "Did you give *all* the keys to Mum?"

"There was nothing in the cupboards, only those screwdrivers and lightbulbs and things like that. And that locked up room is just full of tables and plates and chairs all piled up."

Binny nodded. She had discovered this herself by taking

a kitchen chair outside, climbing onto it, and peering through the window.

"But the big key that I found under my wardrobe said ATTIC. A-t-t-i-K! On a label! I only want to look. There might easily be good stuff up there."

What would be good stuff to six-year-old James, Binny wondered, and while she was wondering James said hopefully, "Presents. Ones that nobody's unwrapped. An Xbox. A proper train set, all laid out. Or just money. Piles and piles and piles of money. And an owl," said James, looking wide-eyed at Binny. "What if an owl lives there!"

"An owl!" All Binny's family knew that ever since she first encountered Harry Potter she had wanted to meet an owl.

"Look!" James held out his left hand and slowly uncurled his fingers. There was the key with its tag, stained old steel, warm and slightly sticky from being clutched in James's hot little fist.

"Come on, then," said Binny.

"It's horrible!" said James, five minutes later.

"Yes it is," agreed Binny.

"I knew there wouldn't really be presents."

"I knew there couldn't be an owl."

They poked around in the dim light of a grimy electric bulb, grumbling to each other, but there seemed nothing to discover. Dirty cardboard boxes. Crumbling newspapers. A stale musty smell of undisturbed dust.

"The air is itchy," complained James, rubbing ferociously at his eyes.

"Don't! You'll make them sore."

"And it tastes," said James. "It tastes of moldy bread."

"You've never eaten moldy bread."

"I have, in the park that I found on a bench. It looked good as new. But it wasn't. It had blue dots on the back. Why are you looking at those books?"

"I just want to see what they are," said Binny, peering at the faded spines. "*Mathematical and Algebraic Functions . . .* Gosh! Yuck! *A Lecture in Mendelism . . . Modern Ideas on the Constitution of Matter . . .*"

"I'm going back down! I don't like it here."

". . . *Dr. H. Drinkwater*," Binny read, while James's footsteps rattled down the attic stairs. "*Senior Lecturer at the University of Oxford.* Probably dead ages ago . . . What's this box? James?"

But James had gone so Binny opened the box by herself.

Butterflies, rows of them, bodies skewered by rusting pins. Fragile colors on brittle, fragmenting wings.

A hand drawn key slipped out from inside the lid. Their names, listed under ghostly outlines, and on the back:

*This case of thirty British butterflies was donated to the collection by Miss Clarry Penrose
(Who also drew the magnificent key!)
July 1913*

Binny looked at the butterflies and then turned to the card again.

Clarry Penrose.

Who also drew the magnificent key.

Magnificent, thought Binny, boiling inside a little. Is that what she thought it was?

A stale smell came from the box. There were gray spots of mildew and sickly yellow stains of damp. Binny thought of the warm gold and brown butterflies that flickered in the sunlight around the blackberry bushes. Those forlorn shapes must also have flickered, until Clarry Penrose . . .

"I'm sorry, I'm sorry, I'm sorry," said Binny, because she hadn't been there to protect them, a hundred years ago.

"Binny!" called a voice from below.

Very gently Binny closed the lid of the box again.

Clem was standing at the open door at the foot of the

attic stairs. It was difficult to know these days just how far Clem had progressed into the distant world of adults.

"I was just looking," Binny said guiltily.

"It's all right," said Clem. "I'm not going to tell you were there."

"It's only books and boxes of junk. And a case with rows of poor dead butterflies all stabbed on pins."

"It's hard to believe people ever thought it was okay to do that," said Clem. "Hurry down to the kitchen, Bin! Gareth's on the phone."

"What again? What about?"

"He didn't say. Just that he needed to talk to you."

"Needed to talk to me?" asked Binny, and tore down to the kitchen and grabbed the phone and said, "Max?"

"What?"

"Is it Max?"

"Max is fine. Listen. You've got to go to that place you were this morning, the exact same spot where you took that photo, and take another one."

"What? Why? Are you sure Max is fine?"

"Yes. Absolutely. Hurry up."

"Now? You don't mean now!"

"Yes I do," said Gareth impatiently. "Go on!"

"In the *dark*?"

That silenced Gareth for a moment and then he said, "Oh. Oh yes. I didn't notice. No. You'd better not go in the dark. Tomorrow."

"I might not have time. Why docs it matter?"

"Look, Bin, just do it. Please."

Summer 1913, Part 4

In the summer of 1913 the national hero was Captain Scott, who had sailed to the Antarctic in his ship the *Terra Nova*.

"And then," said Clarry to Peter and Rupe, "he walked to the North Pole! It took ages. Months! He wrote it all down in a diary!"

Peter looked at her and the corners of his mouth twitched.

"Are you absolutely sure he did that, Clarry?" asked Rupe.

"Yes, of course I'm sure. There's been lots about it in Father's newspaper. How could you not know?"

"I didn't know about the North Pole," said Rupe. "He must have got lost."

Then he and Peter snorted with laughter.

"I think you're both horrible," said Clarry crossly, swiping at Peter and shaking Rupe by his blazer buttons. She herself had cried when she heard how Captain Scott died on the way home, he and his friends in the tent together, with their food all gone and the blizzard outside. "It was an amazing thing to do!" said Clarry.

"Amazing," said Peter, hiccuping.

"Of course it was," said Rupe. "Whichever Pole!"

"What do you mean?"

"Come with me!" said Rupe, and led the way to the sitting room and the old yellowy globe in the corner. There he took Clarry's finger and traced the long downward journey of the *Terra Nova* from England to Antarctica, and the long upward walk of Captain Scott (and his diary) as they headed for the North Pole.

"Oh," said Clarry as she crossed the equator for the second time. "Well. South Pole, then! I knew that really. Stop laughing! It was sad." She looked at Antarctica again, right at the bottom of the world where the spindle went into the globe. It made her feel giddy. She didn't understand how it was possible to live there. Upside down. However, she knew better than to make that remark to the boys. She did say how strange it was that Antarctica was so very cold.

Instead of very hot.

Which was what she would have expected, since it was so far south, and quite close to Australia. Perhaps poor Captain Scott and his friends had also expected it to be very hot. What an awful surprise the snow would have been, said Clarry, if that was the case.

When Clarry mentioned all these thoughts the boys began laughing again.

"I'll show you how it is," said Peter, and gave her the globe to hold, and found a table lamp to be the sun. He was a good teacher. Very soon Clarry understood the coldness of the Antarctic, and could see that it would not have been the shock to Captain Scott that she had feared. She also grasped, as a sort of added bonus, that the universe did not have a top and a bottom and that therefore, whatever the problems of the inhabitants of planet earth, upside down-ness was not amongst them, wherever they might live. At the moment when these surprising facts became clear forever, Peter hugged her.

Afterward, when Clarry remembered it, it seemed to her that there was no end to the laughter of that day. For the time that it lasted, there was no growing up and no grown away from, no leaving and no left behind, no future and no past. It was perfect sunlit present.

Chapter Seven

"Just do it!" Gareth had ordered, demanding his photograph, but there were other things to do too. Binny's family spent Sunday morning at their old house, still covered in blue tarpaulin but with new roof beams already being fitted into place. They had a picnic lunch there, and hot chocolate at the museum that overlooked the sea. Then they inspected the paintings and the models of ships and the things in the gift shop that they couldn't afford, and ran round the harbor for a breath of fresh air and it wasn't until the middle of the afternoon that they left town to go back to the chilly new house.

"Now," said their mother, "I have an extra shift at the old people's home and James is coming with me. Binny, I wonder if you should come too? You could bring your homework."

For a minute Binny was tempted. She liked the old people's home where she and James were teased and admired, given advice and butterscotch, and told stories that only ended when the storyteller fell asleep. But there was Gareth, who as well as ordering, "Do it!" had also (amazingly) added, "Please."

"I'll stay here."

"And behave? And let Clem get on? And get your homework out and do it properly? And sort out your uniform for tomorrow?"

"All those things," agreed Binny, but the first thing she did was collect the mobile phone and go and look for Gareth's footprint.

Which had vanished.

Gareth answered her text at once, with a call.

"What, nothing?" he asked.

"Just mud and leaves."

"You're in the wrong place."

"I'm not. There's a big stone you can tell by. I'll show you. Wait!"

Gareth waited. A satellite above the planet received a picture of a big stone, empty mud, and fallen leaves and bounced it back to earth again.

Gareth said, "That can't be right."

"I suppose footprints do disappear," said Binny. "There's plenty of other giant chicken prints, though. Shall I photo them instead?"

"No."

"They're just the same."

"Except they haven't disappeared," said Gareth. "Are you exactly where you were yesterday when that girl called you away?"

"Called me away?" For a moment, Binny was taken aback, but after all, that was what Clare had done: called her away.

"Yes. Why?"

"I get rid of badger prints when I find them."

"What are you talking about?"

"I trample away badger prints to keep them private. I get rid of them."

"But it wasn't a badger! It was that giant chicken thing!"

"Heron."

"Yes, heron. What are they like?"

"Herons? You must have seen them! Big. Gray and white. Long necks and beaks and lanky legs. Their feathers always look as if they might fall off. Are you going back to the house now?"

"I might explore a bit first."

"Well, be—" Gareth suddenly stopped.

"Were you going to say, careful?"

"Yes."

Bossy, thought Binny, but she was used to Gareth's bossiness, and she soon forgot.

She wandered down the old track, treading gently, hoping for rabbits. There were pink birds about, bright as flying roses, grasshoppers too, like animated paper clips, springing up at her feet. Farther along, by a patch of dark rushes she saw the first heron of her life and recognized it at once from Gareth's description. She curled up in the long grass to watch.

The heron dozed, half opened a yellow lidded eye, blinked, and dozed again. Binny lay so still that a mountaineer ladybug climbed her elbow.

I'm a giant, thought Binny.

Ants, like punctuation marks, wove through the thin grass stems. A beech leaf came sliding down invisible stairs of sky, level after level, slower and slower, and landed in her hair.

That's a wish! thought Binny, not moving. This time I'll wish the perfect wish . . .

She closed her eyes.

The heron woke her. It was the biggest thing she had ever seen flying and it was directly above her head. It was as huge as a hearth rug and it flew like a rocking horse and its legs trailed behind like leftover scaffolding.

It was like being buzzed by a dragon.

It doesn't look true! thought Binny, half between sleep and waking, still rubbing her eyes, and *what is that?*

Not a dog, but dog-sized, not a deer, but deer-silent. A dark shape, dusty bronze, crossing the track, heading for the undergrowth on the far side. It moved very quickly, but for an instant in time it paused, turned its head, and glanced back.

Binny had the impression of great, uncertain, isolation in that glance. In that moment she fell in love.

Then there was a twitch of a dark plumed ear, a silken bound, and the world was empty. The heron was gone. The pink birds were gone. There was no ladybug. There was no leaf in her hair. The air was cold. There was nothing left but an ache of loss, and a memory of a creature more shadow than substance.

She thought, What did I see?

Did I see?

All her life, Binny had seen things where other people did not. A rainy window watched with silver shifting eyes. A blur of color swirled into a person. The light on a wave rolled into a dolphin, or a pattern of leaves took flight. She remembered Gareth's scorn at the Swallowtail butterfly. What would he say about this?

I don't have to tell everything to Gareth, thought Binny. He doesn't tell everything to me. He's making all that fuss about the photo I sent him but he won't say why.

Binny looked at the photo on her mobile phone again. It was so small. So nothing-much. The heron print like a badly drawn star. The tracks of the small mousy creature, and . . .

She raced to call Gareth's number.

"There was a paw print too!"

"At last," said Gareth.

"Why didn't you say before?"

"I didn't want to tell you what to see. You're too good at seeing things that aren't there."

"Of course it's there! What is it?"

"A dog?" asked Gareth, but he did not say it as if he believed it for one moment, and he did not argue when Binny, who happened to be very good at dog footprints (Max having left them all over her heart), said, "I'm sure it's not a dog. What else could it be?"

"I don't know," said Gareth.

At school on Monday, Binny remembered her promise to her mother. At break time she went across to where Clare was standing with Ella and said, "I told my mum I'd say sorry to you about what I said on Saturday. I'm sorry for what I said on Saturday."

"Is that it?" asked Clare.

"Yes."

"I bet you're not really."

"You were spying on me. You trapped me in that tunnel. And you said *'actually'* to try and make me kill you in front of both our mothers."

Ella looked from Binny to Clare in surprise. "Is she mad? Want a chip?"

"Yes, she is. No, thanks."

Ella had an unusual way of eating potato chips. She squashed them to crumbs and then drank them from the packet like a long stream of dirty snow. Sometimes this did not go smoothly and she exploded into a blizzard of salty snowflakes. Already Binny had learned to move out of range when the chip packet was raised. This time she stepped back at exactly the moment that Clare did the same thing, in a movement as smooth as a reflection. They both noticed. Their eyes met in surprise and in that moment of honesty Binny thought of something.

"After you saw me yesterday," she said, "after the tunnel, and after when you were in my bedroom, did you go back?"

For the smallest fraction of time, Clare's eyes remained

on Binny's. Then she glanced away and said, "I don't know what you're talking about."

"Did you go back to the old railway line?" persisted Binny, but it was no use. Ella was now erupting with volcanic force, pouring tears and gasping and staggering about.

"Air!" shouted Clare, and seized her friend's elbow, pushed past Binny, and headed for the door. Just before they got there Ella ceased erupting, but Clare did not stop hurrying.

Binny didn't see either of them again that morning, nor at lunchtime, because she had at last discovered a place where she could have a little peace. This was the school reference library. As soon as she could escape the crowds, Binny slid quietly inside, and tiptoed between bookcases to a secluded seat from which she could see both doors. Except for a teacher invisible behind a mountain of marking, and two much older students toiling over homework, the room was empty. Binny picked up a book, but only part of her read. Most of her listened to the homework sighs, the papers turning, a radiator humming as it warmed, footsteps in the corridor outside.

It was a watchful, jungle peace.

"Still, no one said 'grockle,'" she told Clem on the bus home that afternoon.

"Well, they're bound to get tired of the same stupid jokes."

"Gareth said in the end they forget they hate you."

"They don't know you, Bin, so how can they hate you?"

"You can hate people you don't know," said Binny, who always had been a very good hater herself. "Gareth says if you think about it, hardly anybody likes hardly anybody."

"Oh, Gareth!" said Clem scornfully. She'd never got on with Gareth. He was too arrogant, and too fascinated by natural history. "Why do you know this stuff?" she had demanded of him once, when he had gone too far over a paella and told her everything he knew about the ingredients. "Why not football, astrophysics, Xboxes, Facebook? Why not take up the saxophone? Why not start up a band?"

"Gareth," said Binny, "only likes ten people in the whole world and guess what, I'm one of them!"

"Well, of course you are," said Clem. "If I only liked ten people in the whole world you would be one of them."

"Would I really?" asked Binny, shining.

"Top ten! 'Course you would! Here's our stop! Come on!"

It was one of the days when Clare was also on the bus. Binny had worked out strategies for these times. If Clare got off first, Binny lingered, dawdling, deliberately dropping things, driving Clem distracted but not setting off until Clare was far ahead. If things worked out the other way round and Binny was off first, she abandoned Clem and sprinted. Clem would follow afterward, secure in her almost-grown-up world, impatiently retrieving anything Binny scattered in her flight.

This time, Clare was behind them so Binny ran, airy with happiness at the thought of being in Clem's top ten, plowing through drifts of orange beech leaves and startling Pecker as she whizzed round the corner of the house.

She arrived back to find her mother and Mrs. Tremayne hanging curtains; ancient heavy winter-smelling ones. They were busy in the bedrooms so Binny retreated to the living room, where she found James, upside down in a chair, eating cookies with his legs stretched higher than his head.

"Hello, don't . . . ," he began, his eyes on the television. "Oh, it's you! Look! Me and Mrs. Tremayne have mended the television! Could you pass me another cookie please?"

Binny handed him a cookie and sat down on the hearth rug in front of the electric fire. Cinderella was there, bathing in the heat. "Cinders, Cinders," murmured Binny, reaching out to stroke her and Cinders purred and rolled. She was snow white all over, but her eyes were grass green and the pads of her paws were kitten pink. If they were twenty times bigger, thought Binny, what kind of paw prints would they leave? And if Cinders was twenty times bigger, what sort of cat would she be?

"A jagular," said James, and Binny jumped and looked up from her dream to find that he too was watching Cinderella.

At that moment Mrs. Tremayne's voice was heard outside the door.

"Thinking of your hen," she said, her head appearing before her words, "you might use that little brick shed round the back and put her coop in at night. The door has a good latch, and she'd be out of the wind and whatever. Foxes."

"Foxes?" repeated Binny.

"And I'll have a word with Mark," said Mrs. Tremayne's head, and disappeared before Binny could ask, "Who's Mark?"

James did not care about Mark or foxes. He tumbled down from his chair exclaiming, "A house for Pecker! Her own little house! Come on, Binny! *Come on, Binny! Come on, Binny, please!*"

So Binny got herself to her feet and followed him outside, and there was the shed, a window buried deep in ivy, a low black painted door, and a hundred years of dust on the wide window ledge and floor.

"I'll get a brush and sweep," said James, who loved sweeping, and went scurrying back to the house. A minute later he was raising great gray thunderclouds of dust, while Binny pulled long strands of ivy from the windowpane.

"Guess what somebody in my class said," said James, as he swiped at a cobweb hanging in the doorway. "He said his brother sees jagulars all the time round here. Jagulars and panthers, when he's out on his paper round!" James hit at a cobweb again, missing Binny's head by nearly nothing at all, and continued cheerfully, "They escape out of zoos. They get out of the cages and the zookeepers don't dare tell anyone in case they get into trouble. And then the zoos say, 'Oh dear our poor jagular has died!' No wonder Gertie got got!"

"Who told you all that rubbish?" asked Binny.

"I told you! Somebody in my class. Nobody you know."

"Oh, them," said Binny rudely. Somebody-in-my-class and Nobody-you-know had been two good friends of her little brother ever since he started preschool, aged three. They seemed to move around with him, changing school when he did. They both led, according to James, exciting and privileged lives. No one in the family had ever met them.

"It's true," insisted James. "I told you before that it was a jagular got Gertie. That's why I didn't want to go and look for her with you. Because of danger."

The whole conversation was making Binny more and

more uneasy. Ever since the shattering moment when she had fallen in love with her shadowy animal, she had understood completely why Gareth trampled his badger prints to hide them from curious eyes. Secret was safe, said Gareth, and he was right.

Binny changed the subject from paperboys and their early morning illusions.

"I've got this window clear. What's it like inside now?"

"Come and see."

"Not till you've put that brush down!"

James lowered his weapon, and Binny stepped cautiously through the door and looked around. Flaking whitewashed walls. A wide shelf under the window. So many cobwebs that they entirely veiled the ceiling.

"Imagine it in the dark!" she exclaimed. "Shut your eyes!"

James shut his eyes and invisible spiders trickled down his neck. He squirmed and wriggled. "Pecker won't mind, though," he said. "She likes spiders. She gobbles them up! Let's go and get her and show her her new house."

Pecker squawked with dismay when James and Binny lifted the hen coop, but once inside the shed she didn't seem to mind. They arranged her so that she had a view from the window, and gave her an extra supper to make up for the disturbance. A family of sparrows were chattering in the ivy and Pecker crooned back to them as she picked up her corn.

"They can be friends," said James, pleased.

Binny looked around one last time before they closed the door. In a corner of the windowsill something caught her eye. It was a rectangle of cardboard, yellow with age and gray with dust, tucked almost out of sight. As soon as she picked it up she recognized the handwriting.

She took it in to show to Clem.

"It's that Clarry again," she said. "The one who did the butterflies." Clem had seen the butterflies for herself now, and she hadn't liked them any more than Binny had, although she had pointed out how carefully the little key was drawn. Now she read:

Web of Common House Spider
(*Tegenaria domestica*)
August 1912

"Goodness!" said Clem, shuddering.

"It was right beside a real cobweb," said Binny. "Well, a lot of real cobwebs; there's millions in that shed! It must have been there for a hundred years. Read the back!"

Clem turned it over and read,

The Museum of the Penrose Cousins
A World Famous Collection from All Over the World
Collected by
Rupert Penrose
Peter Penrose
Clarry Penrose

"It must have been a sort of game they played," said Clem. "Now come and see what I found! It fell out of one of those old books."

It was a cardboard photograph folder with writing inside.

Clarry, Rupert, Peter
August 1913

"There they are," said Clem, holding it out to Binny. "Peter looks as sulky as Gareth, but Rupert looks nice. Grown up, compared to the others. I wonder what happened to him, nineteen thirteen . . ."

But Binny was looking at Clarry, gazing at her with great dislike.

"All those butterflies," said Binny.

Three figures in a brown damp speckled photograph. A tall fair boy in the center, squinting cheerfully into the camera, a small dark girl with raggedy hair, and an equally dark and untidy boy. The girl was not looking at the camera. She was gazing worriedly across to the boy on the other side. He was glaring straight ahead, arms folded, enduring it. *Smile!* someone must have said, and the fair boy had grinned, the girl's eyes had opened wide, and the breeze had lifted the dark boy's hair into a lopsided ruffle.

Summer 1913, Part 5

Captain Scott's ship, the *Terra Nova*, was back from the Antarctic. The newspapers were full of pictures.

Peter said he didn't see what all the fuss was about.

"Why is everyone so shocked that they died?" he asked. "I'm not surprised at all."

"Peter!" said Clarry.

"It happens," said Peter. "People die. You don't have to go to the Antarctic to do it. If they" (that was his father and his grandfather, both very enthusiastic and ganged up against him) "make me go to that boarding school, I'll die."

"What of?" asked Clarry practically.

"Of nothingness," said Peter.

"What?"

"Nothingness! Nothingness! Nothingness!" shouted Peter. "I'll die because there will be nothing to keep me alive. Like an animal in a zoo."

"Rupe goes there, and he hasn't died!" said Clarry furiously. "Why should you when Rupe didn't?"

"Because I am not Rupe," said Peter, limped across the room and slammed out of the door.

As the summer went on, Peter grew more and more bad-tempered and isolated. Often he made long journeys alone on his bicycle across the fields and the moors. Now and then he came back with butterflies.

Not always, thought Clarry. And not lots. One at a time. But she sometimes looked doubtfully at her brother.

"Do you find them dead?" she asked once.

"For goodness' *sake*!" said Peter.

So Clarry understood that of course he found them dead.

Chapter Eight

One Saturday morning James came running across from his bedroom to Binny's calling, "Come and look! There is a man with a gun outside our house *now*!"

For a moment Binny's heart seemed to freeze at the thought of her precious shadow creature. When she got to the window she saw James was right; there was a man with a gun crossing the end of the garden.

"Mum! Mum!" she shrieked, and her mother came hurrying. She was too late to see the man anymore, but she guessed who it was: Mrs. Tremayne's son, Clare's grown-up brother . . .

"Mark?" asked Binny, remembering Mrs. Tremayne the week before, and her mother said, "Yes. It must be. Mark."

Later he knocked at the door.

The Cornwallises were a town family. Not one of them had ever seen a real-life gun before. They stared and forgot to speak. The gun's owner had to begin. He said calmly, "Mum asked me to take a look around. That be all right?"

"Take a look around?" repeated the children's astonished mother, and she glanced over her shoulder, as if wondering if the house was tidy enough for a visitor with a gun. "Oh no," she exclaimed, suddenly very emphatic, as if she'd decided it wasn't. "No thank you! No! There's no need for that!"

"You've had trouble with your hens?" said their patient (but armed) visitor, and there was a gun-stunned pause. Binny found out afterward that she was not the only one who had assumed Mark was offering to dispatch their troublesome hens. Poor Pecker, surrendering, wings in the air . . .

It was James who first began to try to unravel things. "He means chickens," he murmured. "Some people say hens. What they mean is chickens. Gertie and Pecker."

"Didn't you lose one?" asked Mark.

"Gertie," said James. "All except some feathers. We found a lot of feathers. A mouthfu . . ."

He stopped in surprise at the sight of Binny's blazing green eyes.

"Did you want to come in?" asked the children's mother, suddenly seeming to wake up to the fact that she might be being rude. "I'm afraid I'll have to ask you to . . ."

Binny saw her glance at the gun, and knew she wanted to say, *leave your weapon at the door*, and couldn't because of how completely ridiculous it would sound.

But Mark didn't want to come in. He backed away gently, as if trying not to alarm them, saying he'd just stopped at the door in case they noticed him around.

"Mark!" said the children's mother, when he'd gone. "Goodness me! What was he thinking of? Why on earth would he turn up here with a gun?"

"I didn't know guns were as big as that," said James.

"Neither did I!" agreed his mother. "I'm surprised it's allowed! Does Mrs. Tremayne know . . . She must, I suppose." She paused to look out of the kitchen window. "There he is, across the field, and his sister with him too."

"Clare?" asked Binny, and looked herself and saw that her mother was right. Mark was no longer alone. Clare was running beside him, looking very cheerful, waving her arms as she spoke.

"I suppose it must be safe," said Binny's mother, but she sounded very doubtful.

A Man with a Gun, wrote James in his newsbook that night, *Cam to awer Hose.*

★ ★ ★

They saw Mark two or three times after that, walking the fields in the dusk or the early morning. Always with his gun. Always with Clare.

"I like him," said James, coming in to breakfast one morning very wet around the ankles from the long, soaking grass. "Only he wouldn't give me a go with his gun, not even to point in the air. Not even one bang."

"I should hope not too!" exclaimed his horrified mother.

"He doesn't really shoot things," said James reassuringly, as he began to scoop up cornflakes. "I asked him, 'Do you really shoot things, or do you just have a gun to bang?' And he said, 'However did you guess?' and he winked to show it was true."

Binny wanted so much to believe this that she found she almost could.

"What else did he say?" she asked.

"He said did I like mushrooms because he'd found some mushrooms," said James, now gulping orange juice. "And I said no because they are like cooked slugs. And he said he wouldn't bother shooting any for my breakfast, then. That was a joke. And I said what else did he shoot and he told me apples and oranges and carrots if they ever fly past. He's nice. He's my friend."

"James, I will not have you out with Mark and his gun,"

said his mother very firmly. "However nice he is. Whatever he says."

James stuck out a mutinous lip, but found it was no use. His mother was crashing together breakfast things in one of her rare bad tempers. "Guns!" she said. "Of all the unnecessary, destructive . . . What is it about boys and guns, for goodness' sake?"

"Girls too," said Binny, thinking of Clare, always tagging on.

"I don't know what's the matter with people!" continued her mother. "And as for saying he just has it to bang! Although, perhaps . . . Do people do that, do you think, just have them to bang? I suppose that's all you'd need, a bang . . . Oh hello, Mrs. Tremayne!"

For Mrs. Tremayne had appeared, as unnervingly as usual, and as usual she began in the middle of what she wanted to say.

"Appled out!" she announced. "Yes, hello, good morning. There's apple trees forever at our place. We're appled out this year. And last year hardly a handful and you can't blame the frost because we hadn't any. I brought a few," she added, and nodded toward the doorstep.

Four bulging carrier bags had materialized there. A cake was balanced on the top of one of them.

"Apple cake," said Mrs. Tremayne. "I like to leave a cake for guests. There you are. A pleasure."

She was gone. Binny and her mother looked at each other and then at the four enormous bags of apples.

"There must be a tree full!" said Binny.

"She is a truly kind person," said Binny's mother. "This apple cake is still warm. She must have been baking at dawn. There are more apples there than I buy in a year!"

They ate apples on the way to school that day, there were apples in all the lunch boxes, and an extra bag for James to give out to his friends. There was apple cake waiting when they got home from school. It was heavy and scented, buttery sweet with a cinnamon crisp top. Binny ate a slice and it was wonderful. She took a second outside, and wandered through the thick grass to the end of the garden, thinking about Mrs. Tremayne. Definitely not a witchy old woman, she decided, feeling rather ashamed. Fierce when it came to protecting her cupboards and her beds, but certainly a wonderful cook. And there had been chocolate for James, and a house for Pecker, as well as hot water bottles and bus timetables.

Binny had to admit it; she had been wrong about Mrs. Tremayne.

Mark was nice too. Funny and kind with James, and polite to her mother. There was the gun, but Binny, crunching sugar crystals and cinnamon, now understood that it was only needed for its bang. After all, the Tremaynes kept sheep. Obviously foxes needed to be shooed away from lambs from time to time. A bang would do that, she supposed, better than shouting.

Binny looked down toward the old railway cutting and thought of whatever might or might not be hiding there.

Perfectly safe, she thought, and licked the last golden crumbs from her fingers.

Who was that?

It was Mark, striding across the fields toward her. Mark, with no Clare attached. Mark smiling. Mark with his gun and something very large and dark in his hand.

Binny found herself running, scrambling over the tumbled stone wall, pelting toward him.

It was a bird; a rook. Mark held it by its clenched dark feet and its wings fell like stiff black banners to the ground. Its eyes were half open, heavy lidded and still bright, as if considering its fallen life.

"Hi," said Mark breezily, but his smile had become a little uncomfortable and he glanced away from Binny's eyes. "It's a rook," he said, as if giving a reason.

"But," said Binny, appalled and bewildered. "What happened? Was it an accident? You told James you just banged. We all thought . . . Why? Why?"

She stopped. There was no sound. The wind did not blow. Dark red blood hung from the iron beak but did not drop. Binny's gaze was locked on the rook in Mark's hand. It seemed more than a bird. Iron and silk. Huge. Magnificent.

"What had it done?" she whispered, and she braced herself to hear what this rook, this unfurled bird of wild flight and darkness and leaking crimson had done to be blasted so far from existence.

"Well, it's a rook," said Mark again, and he shuffled helplessly, shifting the weight of the gun under his arm. "Vermin!" he said suddenly, and flung the rook far away, over the wall toward the blackberry bushes.

Binny's head hit him so hard that he doubled up, choking. Her hands clawed his face and tore at his hair. She butted him again, causing him to drop his gun. It fell at her feet and she seized it and flung it after the rook. It was too heavy and clumsy to throw far. There was a nasty crunch as it hit the stone wall and Mark gave a little groan but his attention was on Binny, and his face was worried as he bent to speak to her. "Did I frighten you? I didn't mean to frighten you. Let's get you back to your mum. Hey!"

Tears streaming, Binny shoved him aside and her very hard and sharp elbow caught him in his eyes. He clutched his face, rocked for a second, and said, "Sorry."

"Go away! Go away!" sobbed Binny, so he did not follow her as she stumbled back to the house, pushed open the door, wailed, "Mum! Clem! Mum!" and fell in sobs on the kitchen table.

Her family rushed to gather her up, moving plates, fielding the remains of the apple cake as she pushed it away, hugging her, saying, "What? What?"

"Mark. That gun. It's not just to bang."

"Oh no!"

"He shot a bird. A great big black rook. Dead. He shot it dead!"

"With his *gun*?" asked James, flabbergasted.

"Yes."

"On *purpose*?"

"Yes, and he threw it away."

"Threw it away?" repeated her incredulous listeners, and from the depths of her unhappiness Binny felt a great warmth growing, love for this family of hers, as outraged as she was.

"Call the police," she said.

James gasped, wide-eyed, but Clem shook her head. The

kitchen filled with regret. Her mother said sadly, "It's allowed."

"Allowed? Allowed?"

"Farmers are allowed to shoot things like that. After Mark appeared with his gun the other day I looked it up to see. Rooks. Crows. Foxes."

"Foxes?" repeated James in a very high voice.

"Rabbits. And other things too. To control them."

The last of the fight left Binny and she laid her face on her arms. Clem rubbed her back. Her mother put a cup of tea by her elbow. James asked, "Why did you let him?"

"He'd already done it."

"Did you hear the bang?"

"No. He was just suddenly there."

"What I'd have done," said James, "is I'd have got there before the bang, grabbed his gun while he didn't notice, and said 'Hands in the air!' and he'd put his hands in the air and I'd have shot him dead!"

On the word "dead" there was a knock at the door. Mrs. Tremayne.

Binny, although her face was hidden, could feel Mrs. Tremayne taking in the room around her. Silent Clem and angry James. Her mother, flustered out of politeness. But also the apple cake, nearly eaten. The smell of supper cooking.

James's homework with its bright pictures. Shoes left by the door so as not to track in mud.

"There you are!" said Mrs. Tremayne, looking at Binny. "I was that sorry to hear you'd been upset . . ."

Binny stirred a little but did not look up.

"It's country!" continued Mrs. Tremayne, almost apologetically. "It's always been done. It's farming. We'd be overrun. Rabbits, foxes, I don't know what. We gave up the hens years ago, for that very reason. That rook. I know, I do know, but we've lambs in springtime. It's no pleasure, but there you are. Mark wanted me to see she got home safe."

"Thank you," said the children's mother, and to Binny's complete astonishment she put her arms round Mrs. Tremayne and hugged her.

Summer 1913, Part 6

"Rupe," said Clarry one afternoon, "there's something I want to ask you."

"Oh yes?"

"If you promise to keep it a secret."

"It's Peter, isn't it?"

"Yes. When Peter goes to school you will look after him, won't you?"

Rupe tried to explain. How little he would see of Peter. How foolish Peter would appear, if it was known he was being looked after. How easily he would survive anyway.

"The first week or two might be pretty bad," admitted Rupe (who had perfected the art of motionless, silent, under-pillow crying during his own first week or two). "But after that you get used to it. You learn your way around. Somebody laughs at your jokes, letters arrive. Before you know it, it's nearly half term. Then it's nearly Christmas. And there's ways of getting on. It's a pity he won't be able to do games."

"He wouldn't have bothered with them anyway, even if his leg wasn't hurt. He never did."

"Well, once he's through first term he'll be all right. Second's better. At least you know what you're in for."

"Aren't you going to do anything to be nice at all?" demanded Clarry.

"It's not very easy, is it, being nice to Peter?" said Rupe a bit huffily. "Look what happened the last time I tried."

Just as he had promised, Rupe had brought home something spectacular for the museum. In the forbidden grounds of a large stone house he had bribed a friend to stand guard while he climbed frighteningly high up a huge elm tree. He had groped and scrambled and balanced and prayed his way up to where the branches swayed against the sky, and the shabby crows' nests hung. There, a few days before, he had located a kestrel's nest. There were fledglings inside; he could hear them wheezing and squabbling but it took several more minutes of perilous maneuvering before he could lean far enough over to touch them. The female bird had returned before he could lift one. She had flown at him with black onyx talons as he reached into her nest.

Rupe had rocked a bit then, up on his perch with his hand dripping blood.

"Hurry!" called his friend from far below, and when Rupe tried to reply he found his voice had turned to a croak.

Climbing down was even worse than going up. The young bird struggled, buttoned under his jacket. His right hand had been viscously raked, and his face too, although not so deeply. He was shaking a bit when he finally reached the ground.

"She just missed your eye," said his friend in admiration.

"Can't blame her," said Rupe.

"How many did you get?"

"Just one. There were four."

"You might as well have taken another."

"No." Rupe tipped his head back to squint up through the branches. "One's enough. Look! She's already back at the nest."

"Soft!" said his friend.

"Oh am I?" asked Rupe, mopping blood with his sleeve. "You going up there for another one, then?"

"Not a chance!"

Rupe had gone home smiling the smile of someone who feels themselves to be everything good: heroic, kind, generous, successful, self-confident yet modest . . .

It was evening when he had arrived back at the house.

Peter was sitting on the doorstep in the last of the sunshine, reading a book. Clarry was beside him, making notes for a letter she planned to forge.

Then Rupe appeared.

"What happened to your hand?" screeched Clarry. "And your face! Where have you been?"

"Up a tree," said Rupe.

"A tree?" asked Clarry. "A thorn tree?"

"Talons," said Rupe, "not thorns. Guess what I've got!"

Clarry shook her head. Peter glared suspiciously.

"Look, then," said Rupe, and unbuttoned his jacket.

It was Peter who spoke first.

"Have you got time to look after a young bird like that?" he asked coldly. "What with all your tennis-muck and new friends and you being so amazingly popular and busy and everything?"

Rupe's grin faded and his eyebrows went up. "Steady on, Pete!" he exclaimed.

"Only asking," said Peter.

"Charming! And what's the matter with you, Clarry?"

Of all the birds that rode the winds, Clarry loved the kestrels most. She shoved past Rupe and Peter, groped her way into the house, and since this year she was too old to cut off her hair, crawled into the cupboard under the stairs.

Even there, she could still hear the boys.

"I don't believe it! I thought you'd be so pleased!"

"No," said Peter aloofly. "No. I'm not pleased."

"Clarry? What about Clarry?"

"Don't think Clarry's pleased. No."

"I thought you could take it back with you at the end of summer. I thought it would be fun for her to look after when you were away. We'll give it to her. It can be Clarry's kestrel, yes?"

"No." Peter closed his book with a finger to mark the place, and began to walk off so that Rupe had to run after him.

"What am I to do with it, then?"

"Put it back."

"Put it back? I nearly broke my neck getting it down!"

"Well, now you can nearly break it getting it up again, can't you?" said Peter.

"Being nice to Peter," said Rupe, inspecting his stiff, raked hand, which was only just beginning to heal, "isn't easy! Neither was getting back up that tree. Peter wouldn't have cared if I had broken my neck, and he took no care of his own."

"Peter climbed with you? With his leg?"

"Like a madman."

"Peter shouldn't climb trees," said Clarry. "He always gets panicky."

"Oh, is that what it was?"

"Anyway you did it. And got down again."

"Yes we did." Rupe grinned suddenly. "And got back to find search parties trekking through the countryside looking for you!"

"That wasn't my fault," said Clarry, who at around two o'clock had woken up in her cupboard, crawled out and gone to bed, all without knowing that not only her family, but also every neighbor within reach, was out in the dark searching for her. She had given everyone quite a surprise when she was finally discovered, fast asleep in the only place where they hadn't thought to look.

"It was very funny," said Rupe. "It even made old Peter grin. Stop worrying about him so much next term, Clarry."

"Can you have breakfast with him in the mornings, and lunch and dinner? Could he sleep in the same room as you? Can you take him round to meet people and tell them what he's good at?"

"I'll do as much as I can without making him look a fool," said Rupe diplomatically.

Clarry looked at him dubiously and went back to the letter she was writing.

"Who's it to?" asked Rupe, looking across.

"Father."

"Telling him about your night in the boot cupboard?"

"It's not that sort of letter."

Clarry's father was a hard person to write to at any time, but this was the hardest letter Clarry had ever written. For days now she had been trying out different wordings and it still wasn't quite right.

It was a letter to save Peter.

The Headmaster
West Woods Boarding School for Boys

Dear Mr. Penrose,

I am very sorry to tell you that we will not have room for your son Peter at school this September.

Unfortunately, a large part of the school was burned down . . . No that wouldn't do, too easy to check . . .

The problem is that we counted wrong when we were checking the number of beds . . . No, no, no . . .

Several of the masters have suddenly left . . . . Perhaps that might do.

He is not the sort of boy who would be happy here . . . That was true, anyway, but was it the sort of thing that a headmaster would write? Clarry shook her head, stared up at the damp patch on the ceiling, and was inspired.

Due to leaks in our roof we have not enough classrooms . . . Wonderful! Roofs did leak. Think of the church; its roof was always leaking! They were perpetually raising money to keep the water out.

Please do not look for another school instead because we will write and tell you when our roof is mended and we have plenty of room again . . . (But of course I never will, thought Clarry.)

We advise that Peter should stay at his day school and live at home . . . Clarry read that bit again, murmuring the words very quietly.

We strongly advise . . . That was better. That would do.

"Very long letter," commented Rupe.

"It's nearly finished. What's your headmaster called, Rupe?"

"The O. F. The Old Fish."

"I mean his real name."

"Nothing about him is real. He's a hollow man. Why do you want to know, young Clarry?"

"I'm writing about him to my father," said Clarry cunningly.

"Oh are you?" said Rupe, grinning. "Well, good luck! His name is Gregory. Dr. O. F. Gregory."

"What would he put at the end of a letter? Yours sincerely, Dr. Gregory?"

"Yours insincerely, more like. Yours unfaithfully. Yours untruly, yours with sincere bad wishes."

"Why do you call him the Old Fish?"

"You'd understand if you saw him."

Yours faithfully with sincere good wishes from Dr. O. F. Gregory, wrote Clarry, and she looked at the words very anxiously for a long time before she folded the paper.

Rupe, who was quite good at reading upside-down writing, reached across the table and laid a fragile brown feather on Clarry's hand. He had made it a museum card too.

One Feather
from Clarry's Kestrel.
Which should not have been taken
from the nest in the very high elm trees.

"I found it stuck inside my jacket," said Rupe. "I'm sorry about the kestrel, Clarry. I just thought it might help. Make him think of something else."

"He says he will die of nothingness," said Clarry.

"He won't," said Rupe. "Not while he has you."

Chapter Nine

Suddenly Binny's mother and Mrs. Tremayne were friends and it seemed to have happened very quickly, and with no reference to anyone else. Binny's mother had not consulted Binny, and it didn't seem likely that Mrs. Tremayne had bothered to discuss it with Clare. One day they were politely knocking on doors and the next they were calling each other Polly and Molly and had maps all over the kitchen table, planning a road trip for when the final child left home.

"But James is only six!" protested Binny.

"Nearly seven," said her mother, robustly. "Anyway, if we're doing China and both Americas we need to start saving early. It's called a gap year!"

"Mums don't have gap years!" protested Binny.

"They should," said her mother, grating potatoes for potato cakes, "every five years, to gather their thoughts, but first we'll pay for the roof! Potato cakes, baked beans, stewed apples with cinnamon! Supper for four for less than a pound! You needn't worry about me setting off round the world just yet, Binny!"

"How much of the roof is paid for already?" asked Binny, beginning to peel apples.

"About a third," said her mother cheerfully, and Binny wished she was rich and could pay for roofs and vacations and ready meals and earrings glinting with diamonds like the ones her mother had worn when her father was alive.

As well as planning road trips Binny's mother and Mrs. Tremayne talked. Whenever Binny heard them talking they were explaining their pasts, each bringing the other up-to-date with all that had happened to bring them to where they were now. Binny learned lots of things she had never known before, such as the fate of the diamond earrings, the last words of her father ("I should have told you about . . ."), the whereabouts of Mr. Tremayne ("You may well ask!"), the price of sheep ("Next to nothing"), and all the jobs her mother and Clare's had ever done to make ends meet (which made them shriek with wild laughter). Binny's mother also told Mrs. Tremayne the deep reasons behind the names of her children being Clemency, Belinda, and James, and Mrs. Tremayne admitted that she had thought of Mark all of a sudden, and had never had a doubt about Clare being Clare.

"Named after a wonderful lady and born on her birthday,"

said Mrs. Tremayne. "And what I would have done without her, I don't know. Him gone and a new baby. '*All shall be well, and all shall be well, and all manner of things shall be well.*' That's what she said, aged one hundred and Clare on her knee. And she was right, in the end. Mark's the farmer his father never was. We rented the land out while he was at college but since then he's took it on. Determined."

Mark! thought Binny, as she listened to the two mothers, now in full duet in praise of Mark. Mark the worker. Mark the thinker. Mark the brave.

Mark and his gun, thought Binny. Even the birds in the sky were not safe, and as for foxes and other leavers of paw prints . . . Binny thought of her shadow creature. If Mark knew.

If Mark knew what?

For the hundredth time Binny tried to replay in her mind the moment on the old rail line when the shadow creature had crossed and turned. It was getting hard to do. Each time the image faded a little more in her memory. By now, if it wasn't for the paw print she would have believed it to be a dream.

However, there had been a paw print. A paw print of a cat. A cat much bigger than Cinders.

A big cat.

★ ★ ★

The next day at school Binny made a terrible mistake. She was in the library at lunchtime as usual. There were the usual hardworking sixth formers, the usual paper-swamped teacher. Binny sat in her corner behind a barricade of books. Encyclopedias, wildlife guides, a book of animal tracks and signs. On the library table beside her was the family mobile phone. Binny was being a research student. She had already dismissed every big cat she had ever heard of, including the jagulars and panthers that the paperboy met so often. They were all too dark, or too spotty, or too brightly colored.

And too big, thought Binny, although it was a big animal. Easily as big as Max, and its coat, although not spotty, had been definitely marked. Leopards were spotty, and so were cheetahs and jaguars. What would a baby one of those look like? A grubby baby cheetah? A small muddy leopard? Binny was in the middle of these thoughts when something happened.

A swift hand reached over her shoulder and lifted the phone.

Binny jumped and grabbed. The teacher stood up. The sixth formers stared.

Then the phone was replaced again, as neatly and lightly as it had been picked up.

Clare and Ella closed the library door and vanished.

The heron print photograph, with the paw print underneath, had been on the screen a minute before. Now it was gone.

"Gone!" wailed Binny, abandoned her table, and tore out of the room.

Clare and Ella were gossiping amongst the crowds in the foyer. Binny hurled herself into the middle of them.

"You deleted it! There was a picture on my mobile and you deleted it!" she stormed.

"Oh Clare, did you actually?" asked Ella, and doubled over laughing.

"Stop it!" said Clare. "I mean, actually stop it, Ella! Take Belinda seriously. (It's Binny, actually.) Tell us about this picture, Binny. It must be, I mean, must have been, very, very special."

At once the surrounding crowd began to speculate. What was it? they asked. Binny's boyfriend? Binny's mummy? Binny's teddy bear? Binny's name and address and a picture of her house in case she got lost . . .

"SHUT UP!" raged Binny. "Ask Clare! She knows what it was!"

"I do?" asked Clare casually, but her eyes on Binny's were anything but casual. They were warning Binny to say no more.

Binny ignored the warning.

"My paw print! You deleted my paw print! You know you did!"

Clare's eyes now were horrified, and for a moment Binny was horrified herself. Despite all Gareth's warnings, she had told.

Ella saved her.

"Oh!" she said, like she had suddenly understood something. "That's what you were doing with all those animal books! Looking for paw prints! Jagulars!"

"What?"

"Your little brother was talking to Clare's mum. About the jagulars he believes in. They eat chickens, don't they, and paperboys? And you were looking them up!"

"But what's a jagular?" demanded someone. "I mean, what actually is a jagular?"

"Ask Big Cat Binny," said Clare.

Mark had a black eye. Binny met him in town, quite by accident. To spare her feelings he turned his face sideways and shielded it with one hand, like a person staring into bright light.

Clare made no effort to spare Binny. Exactly the opposite. With no more than one small lost picture on a mobile phone, and James's rash discussions of jagulars, she thought up a new and terrible torment.

Big cat footprints tracked Binny down.

Huge ones, small ones, clumsy ones, careful ones, scribbled in invisible moments on her school books, slapped heavily and muddily across the shoulders of her jacket. They appeared on her desk and they followed her home and sat waiting on her doorstep. They were ink and paint and mud and white dust. Nowhere seemed safe. One evening she found a crimson line of them printed along her bedroom windowsill and on the ground underneath was the stamp that had been used to make them, a coffee jar lid with sponge shapes glued on the top. The paint was still wet. Binny tried an experimental paw print on her arm and saw how easily it was done.

"Very neat!" said Clem. "But why?"

"It's Clare," growled Binny. "Because of James talking about jaguars . . ."

"Jagu*lars*," said James, who in one unsupervised minute with the coffee jar lid had begun a trail of paw prints right over the car. "*Lars!* That's what they say at my school . . ."

"James Cornwallis get off that car *now*!" ordered Clem.

James added three more prints to complete the chain and slid off looking very pleased with himself. *"Jagular!"* he said.

"There's no such thing!" said Clem.

"Oh yes, there is!" contradicted James. "Ask anybody in my class! Ask the boy with the brother with the paper round!"

"Who's he?"

"Nobody you know."

Binny washed away the latest prints as she had washed away many others. Washed or rubbed or brushed or scribbled over, but there were always more to find. Sometimes at school they sprang up in rashes around her. Other times, a whole day could pass with nothing at all. She would relax for a while and then see a dusty shadow on her bus seat or a tiny sketch on the corner of her notebook and they would start all over again.

Clem watched this latest torment in silence. Binny's mother said, "Think of the things you did to Gareth last summer!"

"They were only jokes."

"Well, I think Clare's paw prints are only jokes."

"Is it to do with when you fought Mark?" asked James, catching her in private. "When he shot that big bird and you threw his gun into the bushes! I think that made Clare mad!"

"It's *nothing* to do with that!" said Binny, although when

she thought about it afterward she knew that was not quite true. Clare, Mark's gun, the paw prints, the mythical animal that had silently crossed her world. They were all entwined, and with them came another world: Rupe, Peter, and Clarry.

Clare and Clarry.

It was the same name.

Of course it was the same name!

Binny's mind whirled, and Binny whirled too, up to the bathroom where her mother and James were torturing each other.

"Clare and Clarry!" she said. "No wonder! It's the same name! The same name and the same birthday! The same people, that's what they are!"

"I have no idea what you are talking about," said her mother. "James, stand *still* for *one moment*! I *have* to do this. There was a message from school!"

"Not about me!" moaned James. "They didn't mean me!" His head was green with hospital smelling shampoo. When his mother tightened her grip on the comb she was holding he went deliberately boneless and collapsed to the floor.

"Itchy heads in Class One," said his mother, heaving him up again. "You are Class One! Binny, what were you saying? Something about Clare? Not another quarrel!"

Binny saw the this-is-the-limit-of-my-patience look on

her mother's thin face and came to her senses. "It's nothing. It doesn't matter. Let James keep his nits! He'll just have to stop being a monitor, that's all."

This inspired remark froze James mid-battle. A great calmness filled the cold little bathroom. The children's mother laid down her comb, said, "Wonderful, Binny, thank you," and prepared to leave.

"Stop being a monitor?" repeated James.

"They'll understand," said Binny. "Mum'll write you a note."

"No!" protested James, and grabbed the comb and began raking through his hair much harder than his mother had done.

Poor nits! thought Binny as she watched. Poor nits, poor foxes, poor rooks.

"Why is it all right to kill nits and it's not all right to kill rooks?" she asked, and her mother said, "Not *now*! Binny!" and steered her out of the bathroom.

Clem was more helpful. With her usual clear-sightedness she said at once, "There's killing things because you have to. And there's killing things because you want to. Mum thinks she has to get rid of James's nits. I suppose Mark thinks he has to go round with that gun."

"Clare doesn't have to go with him, though," said Binny.

"She can't be a help. She's probably a nuisance. She must just go because she likes it. And that girl Clarry didn't have to kill all those butterflies either."

"In that picture I found she doesn't look like the sort of girl who would," said Clem.

"I know, but she did. I found even more of them. Round boxes with writing on the lids, round and round in a spiral. Their names and things. I didn't read it all."

"You should leave them alone."

"I only looked for a second. I hate seeing the pins. Have you still got that photograph, Clem?"

Clem unfolded it from a shabby book and handed it to Binny, who bent over it, wondering.

"Do you think they look the same, Clare and Clarry?"

"Not really."

"I do."

"Binny, you can't quarrel with Clare because a hundred years ago Clarry collected butterflies."

"I'm not."

"Why is she teasing you with footprints?"

"Paw prints."

"Paw prints, then."

Clem waited, while Binny wished. She wished that she could lean against Clem's friendly shoulder and tell how it was, right from the first *actually* to the last paw print. She couldn't, because at the heart of it was a secret that was not hers to tell. The paw print under the heron print. The creature she had seen.

Binny imagined the conversation. Clem would say, *"You were dreaming!"*

"Yes but I took a photograph."

"Of a big cat?"

"Of a paw print. Only Clare deleted it."

"It would be a joke, Binny, like all the others."

"Perhaps."

"But if you really believe you saw something we'd better tell someone. The Tremaynes for a start . . ."

It was no use wishing she could tell. The only person she could imagine consulting was Gareth, but he slid away from the subject when later that evening she tried to talk to him.

"Not again!" he said. "Can't you talk about something else for once? You haven't even asked how Max is. He had to go to the vet!"

"WHAT!" shouted Binny, completely distracted. "When? What for? Why didn't you tell me?"

"He's been limping. I'm telling you now. It was one of his front paws. He didn't like putting it down."

"How did he do it? What did the vet say? Has he got tablets?"

"I knew you'd fuss. I nearly didn't tell you."

"HE'S MY DOG TOO!"

"I know. Listen. There was a thorn. He had an antibiotic shot. He's fine."

But Binny wasn't fine and having started her up, Gareth found he couldn't turn her off so quickly.

"If you're not going to look after him properly I'm having him back! It's not fair anyway, that I only have him during vacations. It's not proper sharing. Proper sharing would be if we had him for equal times. You've had him for more than two years. Now I should have him for more than two years . . ."

"Binny, he's all right!" yelled Gareth. "He's bouncing all over. Mum said I was fussing about nothing. Listen to him now!"

Binny listened to a cheerful clatter of happy jumping and barking, and then the less cheerful news of what the vet had charged.

"It worked out at four hundred and twenty pounds an hour!" said Gareth.

"Do you want me to pay half?" Binny offered, frantically calculating dinner money, pocket money, and possible birthday money and trying not to think of her mother's pleasure at supper for four for less than a pound.

"Don't be daft!" said Gareth in the rare kind voice he usually kept for animals, and peace was restored.

They talked of Max, who had shaken hands with the vet. They planned Christmas, when Gareth and Max would be coming to stay.

Only at the very end of the conversation did Gareth ask, very casually, "Does your cat go down to that railway place?"

"Cinderella? She hardly goes outside at all."

"What about James? I mean on his own."

"Of course not! James? He's only six! Even I'm not allowed to go there anymore."

That had been the latest order from her mother. "It's getting dark so early, Binny, and I don't like to think of you wandering about on your own. It would be much less worry for me if you just stuck to the house and garden."

Binny had hardly argued. James's chicken had vanished, and Mark had a gun. Somewhere in the airy autumn darkness there prowled a quiet creature with a dappled bronze coat, sharp black tipped ears, and a profile carved like a small lion's. The best way to keep a secret, Binny knew, was to leave it alone.

Now Binny crossed her fingers, which she believed

prevented a lie from being a lie, and told Gareth, "There's nothing much down at that old railway anyhow. Just weeds and bushes and sometimes rabbits. There used to be butterflies but they've all gone. It's quite boring."

Gareth said, quite calmly and politely, "Yes. I suppose it is. Boring."

He was saying good-bye. He had put down the phone. He was gone, and Binny was suddenly hit by such a gale of loneliness that she could not bear it.

"Gareth! Gareth!" she cried, when her fingers had untangled enough to press the buttons to redial. "Gareth!"

"What on earth . . ."

"It's so hard to know what to do!"

About what? Gareth should have asked. *Do about what?*

But he didn't. Instead he said, "I don't see why you have to do anything."

"Don't you? Gareth, do you know what I'm talking about?"

"You were talking," said Gareth with infinite caution, "about that boring empty railway line."

"What would you do?"

"Nothing," said Gareth. "I'd do nothing. Bye."

He really did go. When Binny rang again he didn't reply.

October 1913

Dear Dr. O. F. Gregory,

I have heard that your school is a very good school. For instance I have heard that if anyone ever seems unhappy or not well then you arrange that their older cousins or brothers look after them. I think that is a very good idea of yours.

I look forward to hearing more good things about your school.

It is very good about the cousins and the boys who seem unhappy.

Yours faithfully,

Mr. S. Smith (Sir Lord)

Clarry wished she could add an address for Mr. S. Smith (Sir Lord) but that was impossible. Would Dr. Old Fish Gregory act upon the idea she had so subtly given to him, or not? She hoped for the best and posted it and began another letter to Peter.

Peter I miss you so much. I wake up in the night and I don't

*know if you are all right. You have stamps and envelopes, why
don't you write. Father says no news is good news and that we
would hear if there was something wrong but I have written to you
three times now . . .*

Even as she wrote Clarry knew that she could not possibly send such an unhappy letter to Peter. She started again.

*I am sorry about all the trouble at the station before your train
left. I couldn't think of any way of stopping the train arriving. That
is why I grabbed your ticket. I thought Father would have to pay
for a new one and he might be so angry he wouldn't and then you
would miss the train and wouldn't have to go. That's why I pushed
it down the drain. The ticket. I didn't know how else to get rid
of it very quickly. I didn't know drain covers just lifted off. I wish
those other boys who were going to your school hadn't seen. When
you said you would never speak to me again I didn't believe you
but . . .*

This letter also was torn to scraps and thrown away.

Clarry spent the quiet October evening worrying. She
worried her way through her solitary toast-and-milk supper,
and then through a twilight wander from room to room

that ended with a long pause on the threshold of Peter's door. She gazed at the empty, tidy bed and thought, it's as if he was never coming back.

Later, in her room at the top of the house, she grew more and more fearful. In her mind she heard Peter's voice, saying flatly and certainly, "If they make me go to school I will die."

They had made him go to school, and since then there had not been a single word.

Don't be silly! Clarry told herself. If anything was wrong, Father would have told me.

Wouldn't he?

The later the night got, the more Clarry wondered. Would he have told her? When did he ever tell her anything?

Never.

That was why, just before midnight, Clarry slid out of bed and made her way down the stairs to the dismal sitting room with the red paper on the walls and the dust smelling piano and the yellowy lamp in the corner where her father sat reading.

"Father," she began bravely, to the back of his leather chair. "I had to come . . ."

"Clarry!"

"I need to know . . ."

"Clarry, what on earth are you wearing?"

Clarry, comfortably and practically dressed in her night things, a warmish red and blue tablecloth, and Peter's left-behind boots, ignored this question. She hadn't made the long journey down two flights of unlit stairs in order to discuss what she was wearing.

"Would you tell me," she demanded all in a rush, "if Peter was dead?"

"If Peter . . . ? Would I tell you? Dead? What silliness is this?"

"You might not. To be kind. In case I was upset."

"You've been reading some ridiculous book and it has given you nightmares," diagnosed her father. "It's my fault. I should check your reading. Tomorrow . . ."

"He isn't, then?"

"Clarry dear!"

"He said he would if he went to school," said Clarry, quivering a bit, partly at the coldness of the night despite the tablecloth, partly at the unexpected *dear*. "He never writes. I've written three times now and there hasn't been a single word."

"I imagine he is sulking," said her father calmly. "I myself have written twice, once to send him some pocket money and a second time to ask if he had received it. I have had no reply to either message. Sulking. Uncomfortable, but seldom fatal."

He raised an eyebrow to Clarry, perhaps hoping she might smile at this wintry joke, but she didn't seem to hear.

"You might write to Rupert," he suggested.

"I did but he hasn't written back either."

"I expect they are both very busy." Clarry's father paused, as if thinking. "Possibly you are not busy enough."

"Me?"

"I have always thought it a pity that you were born a girl," said Clarry's father. "Many things would have been easier if you'd been a boy. You could have gone to school with Peter."

"Girls are just as good as boys!" said Clarry indignantly. "And I do go to school!"

"Miss Vane thinks it a pity that you have so few interests—"

"I have lots of interests!" interrupted Clarry. "I read! I have the museum with Peter and Rupe!"

"Interests that other girls have," continued her father as if she hadn't spoken. "She suggested that you help out with Sunday School . . ."

Clarry groaned.

"Or take music lessons."

"But you hate music!" said Clarry, astonished.

"Your mother quite enjoyed it, Miss Vane reminded me."

"I think I must take after you, not Mother," said Clarry. "Anyway, what sort of music?"

"Piano. Obviously. Since we have a piano."

"Oh!"

They both looked at the silent piano, Clarry's father with a sort of mild satisfaction at having produced such a convenient distraction from morbid thoughts of death at boarding school, Clarry with loathing.

"Miss Vane has offered to teach you. It could very easily be arranged."

"I should like to learn Latin if I've got to learn something," said Clarry.

"I don't think Miss Vane could possibly attempt to teach you Latin. You can practice after school. Before I'm home. I'll see about it . . ."

"No, please!" begged Clarry desperately. "Please not! And Father, about Miss Vane. I have thought of something awful about Miss Vane. Can I ask you?"

"It's midnight. I think that's been enough for one night."

"Father, you wouldn't *marry* Miss Vane?"

"Upstairs, please, Clarry!"

Clarry's father got up and held open the door. He nodded

toward the stairs. Clarry got halfway up and then stopped.

"If Peter dies and you marry Miss Vane I will probably run away."

"I have no intention of marrying anyone," said her father. "Peter is merely being his usual uncooperative self. Now hurry up please, Clarry."

Clarry returned to bed very cold but immensely cheered. She might have to endure music lessons, but Peter was not lost.

I'll write again tomorrow, she resolved. Interestingly. Excitingly. I'll write about natural history and the museum. I'll write him the sort of letters that will keep him alive.

She began the next morning.

Hello Peter. Don't stop reading because this is going to be a very good letter so first I will tell you about . . .

About what?

Clarry bit the end of her pen as she searched through her mind for interesting and exciting news.

Nothing.

She looked out of the window for inspiration. A seagull on a chimney pot. The rag-and-bone man's black and white horse pulling a rattling cart, empty except for the geraniums he sometimes gave to lucky customers. Two cats in the window of Miss Vane's house on the other side of the street, almost opposite, quite convenient for music lessons.

Oh, the thought of piano lessons with the hard fingered Miss Vane!

The rag-and-bone man (who did not just collect rags and bones, but all sorts of odds and ends of junk that people no longer wanted) was right outside the front door.

Her father was at his office. The street was very quiet. Clarry left her place at the window and ran down the stairs.

. . . First I will tell you about the piano, wrote Clarry triumphantly, some time later, *because Father said since we have a piano and Miss Vane is quite convenient she could give me piano lessons and I do like Miss Vane but do you remember how she breathes on people very close, and those little cakes she made me eat that had cat hairs in them, and how she pushes your shoulders with her fingers?*

So I rushed to the rag-and-bone man who was luckily outside and I popped up right in front of his horse and I said, "Would you like a piano?" And he was very surprised but I could tell from his face straightaway that he would even though he said, "And what would your ma and pa have to say about that?"

So I said, "My mother is dead and my father hates music and so do I. No one ever plays it. It smells of dust and fish."

"It'll be damp," said the rag-and-bone man. "That's the glue, smells of fish. Damp piano's not worth nothing."

But he stayed sitting there on his cart, so I knew he still wanted it, so I said he could have it for nothing and perhaps he could dry it and get rid of the damp, and he said, "Where is this piano?"

So I pointed to our door and I told him nobody was in except me.

Then he whistled and a little skinny boy jumped up from amongst the geraniums and all three of us hurried and pushed and heaved and in no time at all the piano was jangling down the road very fast in the cart and I had a pink geranium in a purple pot and a shilling as well for luck.

I have put the geranium in the sitting room window where it looks very nice and the shilling on Father's desk because it was his piano.

Write back NOW! With lots of love from Clarry.

Chapter Ten

Now that outdoor exploring was no longer allowed, Binny was surprised how much she missed the pause between school and home when something magical might happen. The house was all right when her mother was home, because she had the ability to make the most barren place homelike, simply by putting down her bag and switching on a kettle. However, in the empty stretch of time between school ending and her mother getting home, the house was not comfortable. Mrs. Tremayne was the opposite to Binny's mother. She could make the most homelike place barren, and she had gone to some trouble to do this with her vacation house. Holidaymakers, she thought, were most useful when out of the house, spending money in the town, not hanging around at home, wearing out cushions and using up electricity.

"Some owners leave books and toys and I don't know what," she said. "I make a nice cake that can be taken on picnics."

"You make very nice cakes," James had agreed, and had been rewarded the next morning with what Mrs. Tremayne described as a chocolate brick. Anywhere was home to James if there was chocolate about, and there was a lot of chocolate to a chocolate brick—a solid chocolate covering, with fudge underneath. James was sprawled on the sitting room floor eating it when Binny got home from school. "Play with me!" he begged as soon as he saw her.

"Play what?"

"Farms and jagulars."

"Not just now," said Binny, and she took herself off to the kitchen, which was the only other warmish room in the house. Clem was there, with her flute.

"Flutes," said Binny, "are loud. They don't look loud. They look like they'll be all silvery and moonlighty. But they're not. They're really loud."

Clem passed her a piece of chocolate brick and took no notice. When it came to flute practice she was quite ruthless. She did at least two hours a day, and she did it in the kitchen because she needed warm hands.

So Binny wandered the house, and ended up in the attic with an old cardboard box.

Stones, fossils, shells, and other jumble, and yellowy hand-written labels.

Swapped for the pen Peter
had from Clarry on his birthday

The grass snake skin made Binny jump, coiled up like the ghost of a snake in a battered cookie tin.

Found by Rupert Penrose
amongst the reeds beside the river

and:

Skull and wing feathers of male Kestrel
(*Falco tinnunculus*)
July 1912

Found by Clarry Penrose on the tideline
(but Rupe picked it up)

But there was no skull in the box; only the card was left. Perhaps, thought Binny, it was a drawing of the same skull that James had found when they first arrived. Perhaps Clarry had drawn it, and James had colored it in. With that thought, the hundred-year-old chasm between the two times shrank to a space that was small enough to step.

Briefly Binny crossed and joined Rupe and Clarry on the tideline. Clarry pointed to something. Rupe picked it up. He didn't seem to mind picking things up; it was he who had found the snake skin too.

However, Peter had skinned the mole.

Skin of Common Mole

(*Talpa europaea*)

Taken from the molecatcher's gibbet pole

August 1912

Binny knew that Peter had skinned the mole because it said so on the back of the card.

Peter took the skin off the mole.

He did it all and said he did not mind.

Afterward the smell would not wash off his hands.

Binny wrinkled her nose, retreated swiftly back to her own world, and stirred through the box again. A bright blue feather, barred with gray. A once white tennis ball with no bounce left. Some stumps of pencil, sharpened so often that there was nearly nothing left to hold. A postcard of Plymouth Harbor.

My Dear Peter and Clarry,

    I shall be engaged on Friday when you arrive back in Plymouth. However, Miss Vane has kindly agreed to meet your train.

    I trust that on this occasion you will give her no trouble.

    With good wishes for a safe journey,
your father, A. Penrose

What a strange way for a father to write to his family, thought Binny, and who was the sometimes troubled Miss Vane? Here she was again, on another postcard. Purple roses on a dark brown background, and *Birthday Thoughts* in curly writing.

For Clarry,
With kind regards on her birthday,
Sincerely, Alice D. Vane

Binny was fascinated by these glimpses into a different world, where fathers sent good wishes but not love, moles were hung on a gibbet pole, pencils cherished to the last uncomfortable inch, and Birthday Thoughts were purple roses and sent with kind regards. She even forgot the murdered butterflies for a moment to think, Poor Clarry.

This moment passed when she read:

One Feather
from Clarry's Kestrel.
Which should not have been taken
from the nest in the very high elm trees.

Binny ran down the attic stairs and straight into Clem who had come up to put her flute away.

"She took a kestrel from its nest!" said Binny.

"Mind my flute," said Clem, "if you value your life! Who took what?"

"That Clarry! A kestrel!"

"Remind me what a kestrel is?" said Clem placidly, in her room now, polishing her flute with the old silk rag that she kept for that purpose only.

"A bird! They have nests in elm trees. Very high. They have sharp hooky beaks like the picture James colored. And that girl took one from its nest! How horrible is that?"

"Hmmm." Clem picked up the old photograph of Clarry, Rupe, and Peter. There was Clarry in her bunchy dress. It came well past her knees. Underneath, the drooping hem of a white petticoat could clearly be seen. "Fancy," said Clem.

"She made it to the top of a very high elm tree dressed like that!"

"She must have had some other clothes," said Binny.

"Perhaps," said Clem doubtfully. "I bet they were pretty much the same, though. You know what Binny, I don't believe she climbed to the top of a very high elm tree and took a bird with a sharp hooky beak from its nest! Do you, really? Or do you just want to believe it?"

"It says," said Binny, brandishing the card, "*Clarry's* kestrel *from* the nest *in the elm trees!*"

"But it *doesn't* say," said Clem, "that Clarry took it."

It was turning into an interesting day for James. In the morning the chocolate brick. In the afternoon, the discovery of Pecker sitting on a record-breaking three eggs (one added by Binny early that morning, one warm and new laid, and one that looked like a perfect brown egg, except that it was made of rubber and bounced). A final surprise came in the evening, when he and Binny were carting Pecker off to bed for the night. Large pink paw prints all over the shed.

"They go right up to the roof!" exclaimed James, delighted, and so they did, under the windowsill, across the door and over the roof, as bright as a chain of roses.

"Don't they look real?" said James admiringly, but Binny could not reply. Her heart was pounding with alarm, and her eyes could not stop staring at the long deep claw marks, gouged like train tracks, that ran from the height of James's shoulders to the bottom of the door.

They looked terribly real. When Binny touched them they felt terribly real.

"Evening James!" called a voice from out of the shadows. "Need a lift with that coop? How's your hen today?"

It was Mark. He had come down the road on his motorbike and left it by the side of the house to speak to them. One look at his confident grin explained the third miraculous egg.

"Three eggs!" James told him proudly. "One white, one still warm, and one that bounces!"

Mark looked down at Pecker in mock surprise and said, "She lays eggs that bounce?"

"Did you put it there?" demanded James.

"Me?" asked Mark, winking at him. "I've been working all day. Whatever has happened to that door?"

"Clare," said James. "She does it loads. It's because of the jagular. Can I have a go on your motorbike?"

"Because of the what? No you can't!"

"Just for one minute," said James, sidling over. "Only

to sit on," he added, sitting. "Not to touch the key," he explained, reaching out and touching it.

"Get down off there! What would your mum say?"

"She'd say be careful. I am being careful."

Mark could deal with a lot of things: guns, sheep, pub quizzes, motorbikes, bills, broken walls, and the constant repairing of ancient vehicles were all on his list of what he could manage.

But Mark had never tried to manage anything as persistent as James.

"Could I have one try-on of your leather jacket?" begged James.

"Flipping heck!" exclaimed Mark, and he looked at Binny for help but she avoided his eye.

"One?" asked James wistfully.

"Oh, all right, in a minute! Just let me have a proper look at this shed door."

"I've found the horn," said James, deafeningly proving this. "Is that where the gas goes? If you undo it can you see it inside? Oh, thank you!"

Mark's jacket engulfed James so that for almost a minute he was speechless. "I don't suppose . . . the helmet . . . ," he asked when he came up at last for air.

The helmet extinguished him at last. He squawked and

slid to the ground and Binny heaved him up and untangled him, while Mark lifted Pecker inside the shed, closed the door, and ran his hand over the ridged claw marks exactly as Binny had done.

"It's just a joke," said James. "Magic paw prints. Clare makes them. She's done loads, hasn't she Binny?"

"Yes loads," said Binny, beginning to retreat backward to the house. "Hurry up and come in now, James. Supper! Aren't you hungry?"

James, who was always hungry, was distracted at once. He overtook Binny at the door, dodged Clem, was fended from the fridge, the cookie tin, and the cheese, but settled down with a banana to torture everyone with his reading book while Binny helped her mother fry apple slices with butter and brown sugar and lemon and fold them into pancakes.

The awfulness of James's reading book, *My Book of Farm Machinery* ("Why, why, why?" moaned his family, who had already endured *My Book of Road Transport*, *My Book of Bridges*, and *My Book of Weather*), the success of the pancakes, and the inexplicably huge amount of spilled flour and milk and egg that needed clearing up afterward, all distracted Binny from thinking of Pecker's shed door. However, much later she remembered and braved the dark to tiptoe outside to look at it again.

"Don't let me startle you!" said a voice behind a sudden huge flashlight, and there was Mark coming toward her.

"I wanted to double-check it was fastened," he said in explanation. "We don't want any more hens going missing. It looks to me like there's a big rogue fox around. I know Clare put those daft footprints there, but I can't believe she did all the rest."

"Those scratches were . . . were me!" said Binny, stammering with nervousness. "I'm sorry. It was an accident. The door was jammed and I tried to unjam it with a . . . with a . . . fork!"

"A *fork*?"

"A dinner fork!" said Binny, her face burning with lies. "And my hand slipped. Kept slipping, I mean. Don't point the flashlight at me! I was going to paint the scratches out again to make it smooth. I'm good at painting. Me and Clem painted our whole house in the summer."

"And you came out just now to check the color you'd need?" suggested Mark.

"No! Yes!"

"Well, that's funny," said Mark, "because ten minutes ago I said to Clare, 'There's some funny marks on that shed door across at the other place. Where James has his hen.' And Clare said, 'They're only chalk; they'll wash off.' So I told her I meant these great scratches that you've just told me about . . ."

Binny said nothing.

"And then Clare remembered all about them! How for a joke she'd put them there with a knife . . . It's all knives and forks round here, isn't it?"

There was a pause, a dark pause, and not just because it was night.

"The thing about foxes is once they've found something they want they don't give up," said Mark. He said this very seriously and carefully, as if he was explaining something that mattered to someone very young, like James. He peered down at her after he had finished speaking, clearly waiting for some sort of understanding reply.

Binny said nothing.

"Anyway," said Mark, after the silence had gone on for a while, "Saturday tomorrow! No school! No need to be up early."

Binny was so surprised at this sudden change of subject that she actually looked at Mark properly. Under his leather jacket he wore the same olive green sweater that he had worn to shoot the rook. His black eye had changed color. In the beam from the flashlight, it was olive green too. He was so tall he had to stoop to look in the window of the little shed.

"Your James thinks a lot of that hen," he said. "It was a shame how he lost the first one like that. We felt responsible. We wouldn't have him upset again for the world!"

When Binny went in, her mother was reading a poem to James, because that was his homework, to listen to a poem.

The night will never stay
The night will still go by
Though with a thousand stars
You pin it to the sky . . .

November 1913

Peter at boarding school, walking, sleeping, opening and closing books, sitting at desks, lining up for meals and wash basins and the daily distribution of letters from home, not dead, but numb.

"That cousin of yours," said a friend to Rupert. "Have you seen him lately? Bit silent, isn't he? Bit odd?"

The friend was a red-haired Irish boy who translated Latin for pleasure and played football to destruction. He was a bit odd himself, but not a person to ignore.

Rupe sought out Peter and found him crossing the quadrangle, a damp and sunless spot.

"Peter! How's it going down there in the dungeon? Anything I can do for you? Help dig the tunnel? Smuggle you a file in a loaf of bread?"

Peter looked at him with eyes as blank as hard-boiled eggs.

"Pete, you are managing?"

"Yes, of course," said Peter, and walked away like someone who didn't know they were walking away, like someone in a dream.

"PETE!" Rupe yelled after him (although yelling was not allowed).

Peter stopped, but did not turn round.

"You dropped something!"

It was Clarry's piano letter. Rupe picked it up and held it out to him. Peter took it and put it in his blazer pocket.

"That's from Clarry, isn't it?"

Peter shrugged. He couldn't read letters from home. He could not even force himself to open the envelopes. He could only endure the world he was living in by pretending the one before had never existed.

"Listen, Pete," began Rupe, and then paused as a bell rang. He began again. "Look, I've got to go. You know where to find me, don't you?"

"Yes," said Peter, who didn't know, and didn't care. He had six letters in his pocket now. They made it feel stiff and bulky.

Later he took them out and stowed them in his locker, found himself missing them, and put them back.

He wasn't the only unhappy person in the school. The

small blond boy in the next bed to his said, "I've been counting when they give them out. You've had six letters now."

Peter looked at him.

"Six," said the boy.

"So?"

"It's not fair."

"Oh."

"How long does it take to get letters from Malta?"

"Malta?"

"I've waited and waited," said the boy. He looked at Peter's letters like a dog looks at its dinner.

Peter didn't know what to do. He couldn't give the boy his letters. He couldn't hurry up letters from Malta. He said, "I'll read them to you if you like," and one by one, he opened them.

"Ten shillings," said the boy, when the pocket money appeared. "Your father's sent you ten shillings."

He didn't speak enviously. He was just keeping count. Six letters. Ten shillings. One father.

Peter read on.

"You've got a sister," stated the boy. "Have you got a brother too?"

"No."

"A mother?"

"No."

"A father though."

"Yes."

"*And* a sister?"

"Yes."

"I've got two aunts."

"Oh."

"Two aunts in Malta. That's all. They don't like me but they're stuck with me. Well, not anymore, I suppose. Now I'm here."

Peter read the last letter.

"Read it again," commanded the boy when he had finished, and when Peter had read it again, he asked, "Can I hold it? Just for a minute?"

Peter passed it over. The blond boy held it. Peter held out his hand, and the boy gave it back.

"Where would you run away to, if you were running away?" he asked.

"Cornwall," said Peter.

That was the last thing anyone at the school said to the blond-haired boy because the next morning he had vanished. Nobody ever saw him again. The rumor that he had run back to Malta took a long time to reach Peter. Peter thought of Cornwall, but said nothing, which surprised no one because he never did say anything.

After the disappearance of the blond-haired boy, Peter read Clarry's letter again. That made three times. On the third reading something flickered inside him like a very small glimmer of a spark in a very dark place.

The next day a fourth letter arrived from Clarry.

Guess what Peter! I have been to the library and I have found a butterfly book that I am sure you haven't seen. It is much newer than the butterfly book you took to school. It has colored plates of all the butterflies, the underneaths of their wings as well as the tops.

I wonder where our kestrel is now. I found out what its name means in Latin. Falco is falcon and tinnunculus is because of the word for a little bell ringing in French. Because French people think its call is like a little bell. French bells must be different to English bells but it is a nice idea. There should be a book of what all the Latin names mean. I asked at the library if there was such a book and the librarian said no, so when I have learned Latin I might write one. You can help if you like.

Love from your sister, Clarry

Peter read this letter twice, turning straight back to the beginning as soon as he reached the end. He already knew the stuff about the kestrel's name but the book was not a bad idea. It was a good letter. It made Peter think of the blond-haired boy. He wished he was still in the next bed. Then he could have said, "Do you want to hear this letter from my sister?"

Rupe, wrote Clarry by the same post. *I am sending Peter a parcel but I am sending it to you so that you can see him open it and then tell me what he says. I am sorry if you thought it was a parcel for you and I have made you this bookmarker to make up. Love from Clarry*

The parcel held a round white cardboard box. On the lid of the box Clarry's writing spiraled from the edge to the center. Right in the middle was a tiny museum card.

Large Blue Butterfly
(*Maculinea arion*)

The writing said:

Peter, look! I don't suppose you ever thought I would send you one of these. Look at the blue on the wings underneath. I hope the pin is in the right place. Love from your sister, Clarry

"I'm a bit impressed," said Rupe, peering into the box. Then he laughed out loud and looked again. "I'm very impressed! I'm stunned! It looks perfect. Have you ever seen one?"

Peter shook his head.

"I'm to write and tell her what you say," said Rupe. "You haven't said anything."

"It's a male," said Peter. "You can tell by the size of the wing spots. The pin's not in the right place. Still . . ."

He didn't say anything at first, Clarry, wrote Rupe, under a small picture of Peter in his spectacles turning cart-wheels on the school chapel roof. *But I could tell he was pleased. My bookmark is undoubtably the best bookmark in the school. I have showed it to twenty-three people so far and they all offered me money for it. It's going to be hard to keep it from being stolen. I would never part with it, but if times get hard I may rent it out.*

Do something for me please, Clarry. Tell your father to tell the grandparents that your cousin Rupert will NOT be going to university. I have told Grandfather myself but he cannot seem to understand. "It doesn't have to be Oxford," he says (flinching). "There's other places . . ." (He tries to bring himself to say the dread word, "Cambridge," fails, but manages to croak "London" without actually weeping.) Why is it that no one can grasp my simple wish for no more books and a great deal of fun.

Your admiring cousin, Rupe

"Rupe says," said Clarry to the screen of newspaper that was shielding her father from herself and the breakfast table, "he's not going to university and please will you tell Grandfather."

"Nonsense," said her invisible father, and then after a very long time he added, "Although, I suppose . . ." (there was another almost unbearable pause while he made a very careful turn of a page) "it doesn't have to be Oxford."

"He doesn't want to go anywhere."

"He'll do as he's told." Clarry's father rattled the newspaper back into shape, stood up very quickly, said, "While I'm out please refrain from disposing of any more furniture to rag-and-bone men," and left before Clarry could show him the picture of Peter cartwheeling on the roof.

He is never, ever going to stop minding that I gave away the piano, thought Clarry sadly, but ten minutes later she stopped being sad because the morning post arrived and at last there was a letter from Peter.

Real paper proof that he was actually alive.

Although still grumbling.

Dear Peter, Clarry wrote back immediately in reply.

Your book is very old and I think the pictures in it are faded. Think of Peacock butterflies. Your book makes them look all brownish, when really they are as bright as paint.

The pictures in the book from the library are much brighter than yours. That is why the Large Blue I sent you looks so blue. I thought the pin might not be right. If you move it, be very careful of the antennae. I think they will break easily.

Love from your sister, Clarry

One butterfly, no matter how blue and beautifully labeled, was not enough to turn Peter from darkness to light. There were still days when he crawled out of bed, spoke no words, ate no food, saw no colors, waited dumbly for the dark and another day over. But also there were days when he re-read his horde of letters and inspected his butterflies. A Purple Hairstreak had followed the Large Blue. It was not perfect, but he grumbled less about it than he had about the blue. In his reply to Clarry he actually bothered to draw a diagram of how the pins should be placed. He was definitely reviving. Without realizing it, he had begun to look out of the windows again. There was a morning when he noticed a bird hanging in the air like a balanced star.

"There's a kestrel," he said to the new boy from the next bed, a bony creature with a permanent cold.

"A what?"

"A bird. A kestrel. *Falco tinnunculus*."

"What's that mean?"

"It means falcon that sounds like a small bell ringing."

The bony boy gave a great wet sniff, plodded to the window, stared up at the kestrel, and then looked out across the sodden sports fields.

"Doesn't it ever get too wet for football?" he asked. "Football hurts. Rugby really hurts. Cross-country is agony. You get out of it with your leg. How'd you hurt it so bad?"

"Jumped off a train."

"A moving train? Or a standing train?"

"Moving."

"Did it hurt?" The bony boy seemed obsessed with the word.

"Of course," said Peter.

"Even so," said the bony boy, considering, "it would only hurt once. You'd just have to shut your eyes and do it. And if you changed your mind and didn't want to, you could always go on to the next station." Then he turned his gaze away from the terrible sports fields and looked instead toward the village.

A bell went, the bell for morning prayers and breakfast. Peter and the bony boy left the window and set off down the stairs together. During the day Peter noticed the bony boy looking at him once or twice as if interested in his limp. At nighttime he noticed how very tidy and empty the bony boy's bed appeared.

Like a deserted bed.

At school, Peter had retreated so far into his own private shell that the outside world hardly touched him at all. But still, this bed. What was it about the bed beside his, that people kept abandoning it? The blond-haired boy would be in Cornwall by now, if he was lucky, Malta if he wasn't, but the bony boy with the cold who didn't like football, where was he?

Despite his leg, Peter could move quite fast when he wanted. Down through the school he hurried, into the darkened common room and caught the bony boy, one leg in and one leg out of the window.

"Do you want to hear this letter from my sister?" asked Peter.

Clarry had a list, remembered from summer: A Large Blue. A Purple Hairstreak. A White Admiral. A Silver Spotted Skipper. A Swallowtail.

How did you know he wanted them most? asked Rupe in his letter describing the success of the latest parcel to Peter.

He told me in the summer, Clarry wrote back. *But I didn't even know what they were like until I looked them up in the book. The Swallowtail is the best, but I think it will be the hardest. Perhaps it will be too hard. Or perhaps things will never be so bad that I'll need to send a Swallowtail.*

So the Swallowtail is your final emergency butterfly? replied Rupe teasingly. *The one that you will send to the rescue when the worst comes to the worst, and all other hope is lost?*

Yes, said Clarry. *You know how the globe in the sitting room is more than just a round ball? And books are more than just paper? I think Swallowtails are more than just butterflies. But I expect you will laugh.*

The White Admiral butterfly followed the Purple Hairstreak after an unusually long letter from Peter.

The boy in the next bed had his family visit, he wrote. *They came in their car, his parents and his sister. Vanessa. That means butterfly. She didn't know that, until I told her. They took me out to dinner with them because it was me who stopped him climbing out the window. I had to sit beside his sister in the back of the car. It was even worse than traveling by train. All they said afterward was, "Why didn't you ask us to stop?" But I wished I was dead.*

Clarry sent the White Admiral, and the suggestion that Peter write to Vanessa's family and apologize.

Of course I've already done that, wrote Peter huffily by return of post. *And a postcard to Vanessa, but I don't suppose I'll ever see her again.*

Clarry sent the Silver Spotted Skipper to soften her own bad news.

Peter, there won't be Cornwall this summer.

Chapter Eleven

Binny could not sleep for thinking. Clarry and the kestrel. Clare and the paw prints. Knives and forks and the marks on Pecker's shed door. Mark and his gun. Gareth and his silence. James and his poem that was stuck in her head like a tune.

The night will never stay
The night will still go by
Though with a thousand stars
You pin it to the sky . . .

It was the pins that reminded Binny of Clarry and the butterflies. Every day she was beginning to think more and more about Clarry. The girl with the kestrel. The girl who shared a name with Clare. The girl who drew pictures with the ends of pencils. She was part of the story that held Binny and Clare and James and Mark and yet she was a mystery. She had lived in another world. Binny still had not looked at the butterflies in the round cardboard boxes, nor read the writing on the lids. What had Clarry written there? She had lovely writing, small and even, like a chain of fine dark links. It was writing from that other world, and Binny had a sudden feeling that she should look at it again.

Two minutes later she tiptoed down from the attic, with her hands full of small round boxes.

Five had the spiraling writing on the top, around a minia-ture label. One was white, except for a shadow of scribbled pencil. Binny had to hold it close to her bedside lamp to read it, one word, *Rupe.*

Rupe, the laughing blond boy in the center of the pic-ture. Binny opened the box, and found herself looking at a Swallowtail butterfly.

It was a gorgeous butterfly, not bayoneted on a pin, but with its wings held wide open across a background of a painted summer sky. Binny looked at it for a long time while her thoughts flew around in the night as if the stars had got loose from their pins. Very gently she touched the left-hand wing, while she admired the lemon yellow, the etching of black, the lapis blue edging, the dusty ruby. She tipped it gently to see the underside. The pattern was perfect.

But the body was dark silk thread wound round and round and the right-hand wing was thin pale card. It was a paper butterfly, half finished.

So then Binny opened the others, the Silver Spotted Skipper, the Purple Hairstreak, the White Admiral, the Large Blue.

And they were painted too.

"Go away Binny!" complained Clem. "It's the middle of the night!"

"Clem, Clem, they're painted!"

"What are you talking about?"

"Clarry's butterflies, the ones in the little round boxes. They're not real, they never were, she made them out of paper."

"Well. Good. That's good. Night night."

"I've got them here to show you. Sit up and look!"

"I really, really don't want to do," said Clem, but all the same she did and when she had looked she said, "Gorgeous!"

"They were paper all the time," said Binny. "I thought she'd killed them. Or bought dead ones from someone else who killed them for her."

"Well, you were wrong, weren't you?" Clem tilted the

Swallowtail in its box, admiring the skill of the careful modeling. "You should have thought harder. She was cleverer than that."

"Yes," agreed Binny.

"You'd have known if you'd looked properly."

"I didn't want to. I don't like dead things."

"Well, obviously neither did Clarry."

Binny was silent as this thought sank in.

"I don't believe she took that bird either," said Clem. "And I think that other box of butterflies was nothing to do with her, except she drew the key. I don't suppose she ever hurt anything in her life." Clem put the lid back on the Swallowtail box, and yawned and yawned because she had been up since six that morning. "Shut the door as you go back to bed. Sweet dreams!"

"What? Oh! Night night then Clem. Thank you for waking up," said Binny, and went.

Pretend butterflies instead of real ones, thought sleepy Binny. I was wrong, I was wrong, I was wrong.

Well, she admitted a little time later, I often am wrong. In the dark she whispered aloud, "Sorry Clarry. Not like Clare at all."

Clare and her pretend paw prints, thought Binny. Much

worse, Clare and her own, Binny's, one real paw print, lost the day that Clare reached over her shoulder in the library and picked up her mobile phone. She had wiped the picture and hidden the memory of it in taunting chains of chalk and paint and ink and mud. Why?

To torment me, thought Binny.

But she thought this thought less confidently than she had before. The Swallowtail butterfly on the table beside her made her suddenly uncertain. She remembered Clem's "You should have thought harder."

Binny thought hard for a long time, starting with the shove against the wall the first time she and Clare had met, remembering the dreadful days at school, the girl who had enticed her into the tunnel, the girl who tagged along with her gun-carrying brother at every chance she got. But how else to stop him shooting? How else to take Binny away from a revealing paw print? How better to hide a secret than in a tangle of jokes and paw prints?

It was utterly dark outside. The window was open but there was nothing to be seen except the outlines of trees against the starry sky. Inside there was a great peace in Binny's world because she had no one left to hate.

"Stay safe," whispered Binny, to all foxes and jagulars and mythical beasts that might be wandering the night. The stars took off like butterflies and the night flew by and she fell asleep at last.

Pecker woke her. Pecker squawking, and in moments Binny was out of bed and racing down the stairs. She woke up properly only when she reached the shed door. In the dusty darkness inside, Pecker was frantic with fear.

It was here again, thought Binny. It was here just now. "Hush Pecker," she murmured to comfort her. "Hush, hush Pecker, it's all safe again. What was it? What did you hear?"

Once again she felt the clawed grooves on the door.

Mark believed it to be a fox.

Mark.

We felt responsible. We wouldn't have him upset again for the world.

Saturday tomorrow.

No need to be up early.

Mark had plans for it being a fox, and today was Saturday, no need to be awake early, and who would want James upset again? Not Mark.

Mark and his gun.

Binny understood now all that Mark had not quite told her.

Mark had seen the claw marks as deep as a carved

signature, but he hadn't seen the paw print, nor the tufted ears or carved lion profile. He believed it to be a fox because he couldn't imagine it to be anything else.

Whatever else it was.

Binny tiptoed back into the house and found her phone. With Gareth it didn't matter that it was three o'clock in the morning.

"What is it?" she demanded. "I know you know! That's why you never talk about it anymore."

"You went quiet too," said Gareth.

"You have to tell me now."

"It's a lynx. I think it's a lynx."

"Is it safe?"

"As long as nobody knows."

That was not what Binny had meant at all. Is it safe for me? she had meant. For me to hunt out in this gray dark landscape? For me, all alone, to chase far, far away from Mark and his gun?

"Not that sort of safe," she said. "Safe for . . . for people. If it met them. Or they met it."

"Oh, that sort of safe?" said Gareth, dismissively. "Yeah. Well probably. I think."

Binny sighed with relief.

"Why?" asked Gareth.

It occurred to Binny that perhaps it would be best if Gareth did not know why, so she became very brisk. "Good night now!" she said as firmly as if Gareth had called her at such a terrible time, instead of the other way round. "It's the middle of the night . . . No, it's worse than that! It's nearly three o'clock in the morning! Go to sleep!"

"Oy! Binny!"

"Good night," said Binny.

Then, by the light of her bedside lamp, Binny pulled on socks, jeans over her pajamas, a woolly sweater over her top, picked up her old sneakers and her flashlight, and found that she was trembling.

Poised on her bedside table the Swallowtail butterfly cast a shadow as sharp and clear as a star.

What Binny would have given, for a companion like Clarry.

Or Clare, thought Binny. When this is over I'll tell Clare. Perhaps we'll be able to start again, and be friends.

The idea gave her courage as she crept down the stairs and out of the kitchen. As quietly as she could, she closed the door behind her and looked out into the darkness. Her courage was not so strong then.

She thought, I can't. Not on my own.

Clare's room was the one over the farmhouse front door.

Binny remembered that James had seen her there when he posted his sorry letter. In stories, people threw stones at windows to wake the sleepers inside, but that seemed a risky idea to Binny. Instead she took the brush that James had used to sweep the henhouse. It was long enough to reach the base of the window.

It scratched against the glass and after an arm-aching few minutes a white figure appeared on the other side. It looked at Binny, raised a finger to its lips, and vanished.

Binny retreated to the shadows to wait.

There was not one light to be seen, but the night was no longer completely black. Instead it was the darkest velvet gray. Every star had vanished, except one quite close to the ground. A wavering pearly star that was crossing the garden toward her.

"Clare!"

"Shush!"

"I had to wake you up."

"I wasn't asleep. I was wondering what to do."

"I couldn't think how to manage on my own."

"Neither could I."

They looked at each other. It was hard to release the secret they had guarded so carefully. Clare began by saying cautiously, "Mark's worried about a fox. He says a big fox has found where your brother has his hen and he said it was too dark tonight to do anything about it but tomorrow . . ."

"It's not a fox," said Binny.

"No."

"I've seen it."

"I have too. Do you know what it is?"

"It's a lynx," said Binny, plunging bravely to the truth. "And we've got to move it. Now, before morning. Before Mark comes out with his gun."

"It took me ages to work out it was a lynx," said Clare. "I did it with books from the school library, as soon as term began. I couldn't believe it when I saw you with the same books, spread out all over your table. And the photo open on your screen for anyone to see!"

"I didn't think."

"And then you came down talking about paw prints!"

"Well, you made it so no one would listen if I did. Prints everywhere. Even my bedroom."

"I had to. It made it safer."

"I hated it."

"Sorry."

Binny did not reply to that except to say, "Let's go fast."

They were already walking back along the road, but now

they began to really hurry. "Sorry," said Clare again, a little breathlessly now. "I really am."

"Well I am too," admitted Binny at last. "Especially about your mum. Her birthday cake and the flowers and card. And the things I said. I was horrible."

"Never mind. The tunnel. Your pencil case."

"Ella's lunch box."

They were silent again until Binny asked, "Can we really make the lynx move? How far does that old track go?"

"Miles, after the tunnel, right across the moor."

"Come on, then!" said Binny. "It will be a million times easier with two of us."

"Aren't you scared?"

"Not so much as I was. Are you?"

"Me?" said Clare. "Not really. Not anymore."

They were moving very quietly now, with long pauses to listen, making their way down the zigzag path.

"Would it be better without flashlights?" asked Clare, and they switched them off, just in case. The thick autumn grass muffled their footsteps, and the night wind blowing in their faces meant their human smell went behind them.

"Listen!" whispered Binny.

A rabbit had thumped an alarm. They stood without

moving and heard another and then nearly turned and fled as a pheasant took off with a great rattling screech.

"It's here," said Clare, in a voice that was only a breath louder than silence, and Binny nodded. Somewhere between themselves and the tunnel something was moving.

Together they went forward, pausing between steps to listen. The rabbits made no more noise, but a blackbird scolded, farther down the line than the pheasant.

"It's going the right way," murmured Binny.

"I hope it's all right in the tunnel."

"I hope we are too," said Binny, and felt a comforting hand reach out of the dark to squeeze hers.

"There's two of us," said Clare.

"What if it doubles back and slips past us?" asked Binny.

"It won't pass our flashlights."

They switched on the flashlights as they came up to the tunnel, and Binny saw for the first time the blackened brick and stone, glistening with water, and the stony, gravelly mud of the floor. She looked hopefully for paw prints until Clare whispered, "Hurry!"

"We're not even sure it's here," said Binny, but twenty yards into the tunnel that changed. Her light suddenly trembled on a dappled bronze coat, and then flew wildly in

her shaking hand but returned to find first huge feathered paws and then two yellowy green cat's eyes.

Blink, and they were gone.

Binny and Clare found they were standing very close to each other and their hearts were thumping so loudly that it seemed the tunnel must echo with the sound.

It was a minute before it became possible to breathe again.

"Fast, now," said Clare, and they hurried.

Because there was no light to look out for at the end, the tunnel seemed much longer than it was. It ended almost unexpectedly just at the point when Binny had begun counting her footsteps to stop herself panicking.

It was wonderful to escape the heavy blackness, to come out at the other side and find the air clear and lovely, to feel the breeze and see the beginnings of dawn in the sky.

"Have you ever been this far before?" asked Binny.

"Not by the tunnel," admitted Clare. "Only by road. But I know that there's miles to go yet."

The old rail line was not as deep as it had been, but the sides were still steep and rocky. It still made a hidden track across farmland and wood, and the lynx was still ahead of them. Now and then they saw a swift shadow cross a lighter patch of gray, or heard the crack of a dry twig, or the frightened rush of small birds, disturbed half asleep. They traveled much faster now, but the way was level and easy, gravel and grass-buried sleepers.

"How long can you keep going?" asked Clare.

"For a hundred years."

Clare laughed.

They left the farmland behind them and the air smelled different.

"We're on the moors," said Clare.

Later still, they found the land was opening out around them. There were gorse bushes and heather, blackberry and bilberry. Half a dozen small sheep bolted across their path, and farther away others raised their heads to watch.

"Did you see it, then?" asked Clare.

"No. Just the sheep. Did you?"

"I thought so. For a moment."

There were rocks and deep stony hollows, rabbits on a nearby slope. It was morning, with colors where there had only been lightness and dark. Since the sheep, there had been no sign of the lynx.

Binny rubbed her eyes like a person waking from a dream. "It's gone, hasn't it?" she said. "We're not following it anymore."

"No. But that's all right. That's what we wanted."

"Could it live out here?"

"I think so. Lynx used to live in this country, thousands of years ago. As long as it doesn't come back."

"It would have to come through the tunnel."

"I know," said Clare. "I wish the entrance was blocked. It's supposed to be."

"We could do it."

"We couldn't make it strong enough."

"Mark could. Would he?"

"I'd have to tell him it was open."

"Tell him, then!" said Binny cheerfully. "Tell him you've been through and I've been through."

"He'd go mad!"

"Who cares? Tell him . . . tell him . . . James might go through!"

"That's a brilliant idea. He wouldn't wait a moment to close it if he thought that might happen. Where are you going?"

Binny was scrambling up a slope to shade her eyes and look around. Clare waited until she shook her head and slid back down again.

"Gone," she said, a little sadly.

"Yes."

"What next?"

"Home," said Clare.

June 1914

There won't be any Cornwall this summer, Clarry had written to Peter, along with a Silver Spotted Skipper, to save him from despair. *The grandparents say we are too old. Father says, "Blame Rupe."*

Rupert would finish school that term, but what would he do next? Clarry's father told Clarry that he was the first member of the family for three generations not to aim for university. "Obviously not counting the girls," he added.

"Why obviously not counting the girls?" asked Clarry, and her father looked at her with mild surprise. "Don't be silly, Clarry," he said.

The end of term came.

Peter returned home to Plymouth. Rupe vanished. No one had any idea where he was until a postcard arrived for Clarry. It came from Ireland. ("Ah!" said Peter, remembering the fiery-headed footballer who had won the Latin prize.) *Having a lovely time, wish you were here,* wrote Rupe. *Lots of love and DON'T WORRY!*

In August he reappeared for one day only, having triumphantly avoided university by joining the army, along with several of his friends. Even Clarry and Peter's father was shaken into emotion by this. "Spoiled, arrogant, underhand, ungrateful, ignorant, and ridiculous!" he said.

"He is not any of those things!" flared Clarry. "You don't know him and I do and he is clever and kind and funny and lovely!"

"Let us hope he changes, then," said Clarry's father. "Since I don't see those qualities being very useful to him in his chosen career."

Clarry turned to Peter for help in this battle, and was startled to see his face. "What?" she asked. "What is it?"

A year ago Peter would have said what he was thinking without hesitation, but now he was growing up too. "Nothing," he said. "Nothing to worry about yet."

Rupe was not worrying. He was jubilant. He wrote to Clarry and Peter that he had never had such fun, made so many friends, known a brighter summer.

The grown-ups were not jubilant. The grandparents came to Plymouth and acted like it was the end of the world. It was 1914 and Britain was at war with Germany.

"At war?" asked Clarry. "*War?* Why? Who said?"

Peter explained, "Germany declared war on Russia, and France joined in on the Russians' side."

"Why?" asked Clarry.

"They'd promised. So then Germany set out to capture Paris . . ."

"What for? How could they? You can't just . . ."

". . . and the quickest way to Paris from Germany is through Belgium," continued Peter, ignoring Clarry's protests. "So now Germany have invaded Belgium . . ."

"Couldn't they have gone round?"

"That wouldn't have been sensible . . ."

"Sensible! *Sensible!*"

"Shut up. Listen. Belgium and Britain are allies . . ."

"What?"

"Friends."

"Are we? I've never met anyone from Belgium."

"Neither have I. Makes no difference. Britain has to go to Belgium's defense . . ."

"Couldn't we just not?"

"No. So that's why we are at war with Germany. Do you see?" Peter waited, as once he had waited for Clarry to understand the coldness of Antarctica, but this time she wasn't so accepting.

"Why doesn't someone tell the Germans they can't have Paris? And someone tell the French not to join in with Russia? And anyway, why is Russia fighting Germany? Can't they all just stop and talk?"

Peter said they probably could, but they wouldn't. And he added, surprisingly, that in his opinion Clarry had more sense than half of Western Europe. But, he said regretfully, nothing could change the fact that now Britain was at war with Germany, which explained why Miss Vane had stopped playing the piano in Sunday School (it was a German piano), why all the newspapers had vanished from the house (Father said you'd ask questions), and why the grown-ups were so worried about Rupe.

"But Rupe isn't in the war," said Clarry, baffled but not despairing. "He's camping and having a wonderful time. I had another postcard. He's got lots of friends and that one he visited in Ireland is teaching him how to play the banjo!"

The grandparents and Father are coming to see you, she wrote to Rupe. *They think there might still be a way of getting you back.*

However, before this could happen Rupe's escape from university became complete, because he and all of his bright young friends were ordered to France as British soldiers.

Nothing could be better! he wrote to Clarry. *Bonjour, la belle*

France and good-bye, dusty Oxford! Clarry, I rely on you and Peter
to pass on all the gossip!

"I bet he doesn't even know what he's fighting for," said
Peter.

"He wants some fun," said Clarry.

"There's wanting fun," said Peter, "and there's shooting
people!"

"Rupe would never shoot anyone!"

Peter looked at the photograph that had arrived in the
morning post. It showed Rupe in uniform, holding a gun.
He had signed it, very flourishingly:

Au revoir, mes amies! À bientot! Rupe!

"He thinks he's in France already," said Peter. "I suppose
he won't have to shoot anyone if he can get close enough.
That's a bayonet fitting on his gun."

"What's a bayonet fitting?" asked Clarry.

"It's a long, thin . . ." Peter suddenly stopped. "Well," he
went on, after a pause, "Rupe had better watch out for
German boys, that's all. They might want to have fun too."

"Peter, why are you saying such horrible things?"

"I don't know," said Peter, despairingly. "Because they
are horrible. Because they're true. Because nothing makes

sense. Because everything has changed so fast. It was only last summer that Rupe climbed that tree and got the kestrel."

"He wanted that to be wonderful," said Clarry.

"He wants this to be wonderful," said Peter. "And it won't be. Clarry, write to him if you can. Perhaps it will help."

"It helped you, didn't it?"

"Yes, and your butterflies," said Peter, and he did something he had never done before. He reached out for her hand and held it tight. Clarry held tight back, and then they went to look at the butterflies and it was all right until halfway through, when suddenly neither of them could look anymore, and Peter began to cry.

Chapter Twelve

"Home," said Clare, and Binny agreed, so they turned away from the moor and began to hurry.

The way back was terribly hard. They did it at a sort of jog. Binny had not known feet could weigh so much. The backs of her knees were sore and tight and her shoulders sagged and ached. The tunnel was dreadful, but when they finally emerged it was to a different world. They blinked at the morning light.

"I hope nobody knows I'm gone," said Binny. "I'm not supposed to be here. I promised."

"We did it, though, didn't we?"

"Yes. So, ha ha to Mark and his horrible gun!"

"Mark's gun is horrible, but Mark is very nice. If he'd stop shooting things he'd be extremely nice."

"Can't you stop him?"

"Do you think I haven't tried?"

"Well he won't very nicely shoot our lynx!"

"Or James's jagular!"

A silliness came over them, half tiredness, half relief.

"Will Mark be out now, do you think?" asked Binny.

"Perhaps. Yes probably. Let's sneak up on him!"

"And leap out at the last moment!"

"Howling and growling!"

"If he's there," said Binny, but there he was, zigzagging cautiously down the sloping path to the rail line.

"Let's creep like foxes and see how close we can get," suggested Clare.

They slunk between bushes like two wary animals, except they weren't animals.

They were Binny and Clare.

Binny's brown freckles and seaweed red hair were perfect fox coloring, but Clare's fair skin was as pale as the moon.

"Your face shows too much!" hissed Binny.

Clare streaked it with a handful of blackberries and Binny spluttered at the sight, and then they both got painful silent giggles.

They began to tease Mark. Clare snapped a twig and he jerked to attention. Binny remembered Max, and how he panted with excitement. She crouched low to the ground and hung out her tongue and puffed and tried not to explode with laughter as Mark's head went from side to side, listening.

Then Clare started a rock rolling downhill to the railway track. Mark turned again, and Binny seized the moment to start climbing. She crept up the slope until she was well above Mark's head, made a sign to Clare to shush, and picked two rusty pointy bramble leaves and stuck them in her tangled hair. Suddenly she had ears. The rising sun shone low and lemon yellow right behind her, and she lifted her head and yowled.

"NOOOO!" shrieked Clare, but she had seen the danger too late. Mark fired as she shrieked and suddenly Binny was rolling and tumbling down the slope.

My frend Mark, wrote James in his homework book. *Shot my sistr Binny.*

I mist it, he wrote regretfully.

From the moment that Binny started to roll down the slope, everything changed. It was as if a great, circling wind blew around her, sweeping in voices and people and urgent demands. Binny was buffeted until she could hardly think, and in the middle of it all came Gareth.

"I've been calling and calling," he said very crossly. "And

texting. Ever since it got light. You called me all panicky in the middle of the night and then you didn't tell me one thing more! What happened? Where are you now?"

"In the car, coming back from the hospital. You have to turn phones off in the hospital. I got shot."

"Got *what*?"

"Shot. With a gun."

"Ha ha, rubbish excuse."

"I did! It's true! Ask Clem!"

"Clem shot you?" asked Gareth, sounding very surprised. "I never thought she'd do that! I thought she was just bossy."

"You've got mixed up," said Binny impatiently. "I said, 'Ask Clem,' because she's in the car. Here with Mum and me. Not because she shot me."

"*What* are you telling Gareth?" demanded Clem, turning round very suddenly to look at Binny.

"Just about being shot."

"Oh yes?"

"Not that you did it!"

"Belinda Cornwallis don't you *dare* start telling people that I shot you!"

"I won't, I won't, I'll tell them it was Mark!"

"Binny!" said Gareth in a hushed, urgent voice. "Don't

wind her up! Keep calm and talk her down. I'll call the police for you now!"

"NO!" shouted Binny, but Gareth was gone, and the day grew even more complicated very quickly with the arrival of three police cars, one in front, one behind, and one boxing them in until they stopped.

After this interlude Binny's mobile phone was taken from her, and so it was by old fashioned e-mail that Gareth at last heard the story of everything that had happened, between the finding of the half painted butterfly, and the dawn arriving on the moor. Binny's messages were long, and so were Gareth's questions in between, except for the last one.

So what is it like to be shot?

To be shot, wrote Binny, at the end of that infinite day, *it is like a great pull that jerks you down. Like as if the ground was yanked from under your feet. It is so frightening that you don't feel the hurt until afterward. First you feel the shot and then the hurt rushes all through you like ripples when you throw a stone in water, and you hurt all over, equally. Then the ripples run backward and the hurt is at the center. But my arm was not even broken. There is a big bruise and a long sore place and that is all. And that's because at the moment Mark fired he knew it was me. And so he nearly missed me altogether instead of shooting me between my blackberry leaf ears, which was what he meant to do.*

When I was a fox.

I got very bumped and scratched as I rolled down the slope. Mark was shouting, "No! Oh no!" over and over and galumphing down toward me. Clare grabbed my jacket and stopped me going farther. I sat up and told them I wasn't dead but they wouldn't believe me. Mark kept saying, "Are you sure? Are you sure?" and Clare said, "You are, you are, you know you are! Poor Mark, poor Mark!"

But I wasn't.

Everybody has been very sorry for Mark.

Nobody has been sorry for me.

I can see why this is.

Anyway Mark is all right now. First he was furious and then he was sad and now he is quite calm and not shaking anymore.

Nobody cried when it happened. Not me when I was shot, or Mark when he had shot me, or Clem and Mum when they drove me to the hospital, or James when he found out what he'd missed, or Mrs. Tremayne (although she looked terrible until Clem made her a cup of tea). But much later when we got back Clare started pouring tears without making a single sound and everyone said, "Shock."

"I hate guns," said Clare. "I have always hated hated hated them."

"But you were off with Mark every chance you got," said Mrs. Tremayne. "Chattering and rushing about, getting in his way . . . Ahhh!" said Mrs. Tremayne.

"I've finished with all that anyway," said Mark.

"HAVE YOU?" asked Clare. "HAVE YOU? HAVE YOU? HAVE YOU?"

"Leave the poor boy alone, Clare!" said her mother. "Of course he has."

Poor Mark, he is very sorry he shot me. Mrs. Tremayne says he'll never get over it.

"Good," said Clare secretly to me. "If he does get over it I'll arrange for him to shoot somebody else!"

It wasn't until much later that they asked what we had been doing out so early. We told them about exploring the old railway tunnel and they went absolutely mad. Mark said he would get it closed off as soon as he could manage and James said, "Oh, not till I've had one little look" and that was brilliant because Mark got up straightaway and said, "I'll make a start right now." James wanted to help but Mark wouldn't let him. He said he'd get a mate and do it properly with stakes and barbed wire and if James wanted to be useful he could look after his motorbike keys for him while they were both busy. James has got them Sellotaped to his arm while he makes a reinforced cardboard safe for them.

I have written this down like a story, but I cannot find the end yet because it is all tangled up with other stories. It helps to write it, though. It always helps to write things.

Love Binny.

Binny pressed "send" and the message whooshed away.

Later there was a tap on her bedroom door and in came her mother. She sat down on the end of Binny's bed and said, "I asked you not to go down to that old railway line. I thought I could trust you, Binny."

"You can, you can!" said Binny. "There was a very good reason. You would have done it too, I promise."

"Are you going to tell me this very good reason?"

"One day I will. When I'm old I will. When I'm . . . when I'm . . ." Binny hesitated. How long did a lynx live? How long had it lived already? How long could her mother be expected to wait? Ten years? Perhaps. "When I'm twenty-two!" said Binny. "Then I'll tell it all, right from the beginning."

"What was the beginning?"

"When I saw the butterfly," said Binny.

The railway tunnel was fenced off. Nobody at school said *grockle* anymore. There were no more scratch marks on Pecker's door and she began to lay speckled eggs as well as white ones and brown ones and ones with lions on. James kept one particularly large white one to hatch. At his school the jagular was discarded in favor of werewolves, which arrived in the locality just in time for Halloween.

"Who told you about werewolves?" demanded James's mother rather sternly.

"Nobody you know," said James. "And don't say they are not true because everyone in my class knows they are."

A week later even the werewolves were forgotten in the excitement of Pecker's snow white egg. To the astonishment of everyone, it hatched. One evening there was an egg. The next morning a full-sized brown speckled chicken.

Clem and Binny and their mother looked at each other and then rather worriedly at James.

"I don't believe it!" said Mrs. Tremayne, who happened to be there at the discovery.

"You *have* to believe it!" said James, and held up in triumph the two halves of broken eggshell that the miracle had left behind.

Everyone sighed with relief, and James named this new chicken Gertie, after Gertie-who-was-lost and in time they merged together in his mind, until it was hard for him to tell when one Gertie ended and the next began.

Still, in Binny's mind this was not the end of the story.

Back at the little house in town, the roof was repaired, the ceilings replastered and the walls repainted. They moved back home in time for Christmas and the children's mother became immediately submerged in recipe books, having not only invited Gareth and Max, but also the Tremaynes for Christmas day, breakfast and dinner and supper.

"But we've only got four chairs," said Binny, "and Gareth is used to big houses."

"What matters is that we have eight plates," said her mother, "and three new friends and a waterproof roof. Gareth will squash in somehow or other and Max can fit under the table."

This turned out to be true, but it was still not the end of the story.

When Gareth came to visit he didn't just bring Max; he also brought his mobile phone. This meant that on Christmas day there was a Christmas miracle, and the deleted paw print reappeared. Binny and Clare hung over it, marveling, and the lynx, which had begun to fade into a mythical beast, came suddenly back to life. It was described again to Gareth, its tufted ears, its dappled bronze, its lion head and the silent ripple of its outline as it moved.

"An animal out of magic," said Binny.

Even on Christmas day Gareth could not put up with

this sort of talk. "Either it was real or it wasn't," he growled. "Make your minds up!"

"Real."

"Draw it, then."

"What?"

"Draw it, before you forget."

This was easy to say, but hard to do. Before long the floor of Binny's room was littered with sketches. James came in while they were busy and stopped in surprise.

"That's my jagular!" he said. "The one that I saw running away with Gertie." He picked up a pencil and a discarded picture and added a bundle of feathers, held in triangular teeth.

"I told everyone in my class about it and they all said, 'Yes that's a jagular!' And everyone at home said, 'No such thing!' Binny, you said that, and now you're drawing it!"

"I didn't know what you meant," said Binny. "I didn't know jagulars looked like that. We were trying to draw something else."

"What?"

"A . . . well, a lynx."

"Links?"

"Yes."

"The proper name," said James, "is jagular. Come on! They told me to fetch you. We're all going down to the harbor. Then Christmas cake. Jelly and ice cream. Crackers. And last presents."

Last presents were a Cornwallis tradition, one saved for each person to open at the end of the day. "Save mine," Gareth had ordered Binny that morning, and she had. It was an enormous badly wrapped bundle wedged in the shadows behind the Christmas tree. Now everyone watched as she pulled it out and undid the paper, and it was an enormous bag of dog food.

"Dog food?" said Binny, staring in surprise. "Dog food?"

It was more dog food than Max could eat in a month. Or two months. Perhaps in three. It was enough dog food to last for ages and ages.

"It didn't seem fair for me to take Max away at the end of the week," said Gareth. "So I thought we could swap back at Easter."

So that was Christmas, with the best Christmas present ever.

Before Gareth went home he had to visit the railway line, and see for himself the scratches on the shed door and the butterflies, the real ones and the painted.

"A girl called Clarry made them, a hundred years ago," explained Binny.

"It's a funny name."

"She was Clare really, like me," Clare told him. "She painted them for her brother when he was at boarding school, all except the Swallowtail."

"Who did she paint that for?"

"Her cousin, Rupe."

"Why didn't she finish it?"

Binny thought that when she knew the answer to that question she would know the end of the story.

The Years Between
1914 and 1917

Every Sunday afternoon Clarry gathered up the brightest scraps of her week and sent them to Rupe in France.

Rupe wrote back about the friends he had made and their endless jokes, the Frenchness of French towns, the comfort of hot tea on cold mornings, a little cat he had befriended, the cakes his grandmother posted to him, currant cakes and gingerbread and cherry loaves, just like she had sent to him at school.

Time passed.

Rupe wrote about the summers they had spent together and that Clarry should not worry if sometimes his letters seemed to take a long time to arrive. That the little cat was gone now, and he hoped it was somewhere warm and dry because French rain was wetter than English rain.

Then it was winter, and Rupe wrote that this time last year he had been at school playing football and sometimes when he thought about it it was hard to believe. At Christmas he wrote about how often he thought of them, and he was afraid there wasn't very much news.

After that there was a long break, but another letter came at last. It said, *I'm sorry Clarry. It's all a bit of a mess, isn't it? I try not to let myself think.*

Once he came home on leave. Clarry didn't see him. He went to Cornwall, stayed one night, and left the next morning. His grandparents said he had been very quiet.

"Quiet?" said Clarry.

Life was quiet for Clarry too. Peter was back at school. Her father worked. The news was terrible. There were no more letters from France.

Another year passed.

Rupe wrote suddenly, *Were they real, those summers? The grass and the quiet? Is anything left how it used to be? So many things are gone. Are you still the Clarry who sent butterflies? Or have you vanished too?*

Clarry went to find Peter, who even though it was supposed to be the school break, was working for exams. Peter read Rupe's message, pushed back his glasses, rubbed his eyes irritably, and then read it again.

"He's still alive anyway," he said, speaking his uncomfortable thoughts out loud because it was no use any longer trying to hide the truth from Clarry. "At school there's a list in the entrance hall of old boys that have joined up. And there's another one, all blue and red and gold across the top. That Irish chap's on it and the Head's nephew that people said got let off everything . . . Don't say anything about that to Rupe, though."

"What shall I say? Help me Peter."

Peter looked down at the letter again. "Tell him those summers were real," he said at last. "Tell him how we think of him every day. Tell him you haven't vanished. Make him believe it. He wants to believe it."

He sounded unhappy and he was. Unhappy because Rupe had gone rushing off to France as thoughtlessly as in the past he had gone rushing onto a sports field. Unhappy because he, Peter, could think of no way to help. Unhappiest of all because he had jumped off a train and now never would have to face what Rupe was facing.

"Send him a butterfly," he said.

"A butterfly? To France? A butterfly when things are so terrible?"

"You never sent a Swallowtail."

"I was saving that, for in case."

"Now it is in case," said Peter.

It took more than a single day to make a butterfly. The bodies were always the hardest parts to do. Clarry shaped matches to the right length and then wound them with thin fine silk, black, deep brown, and deep gray, layer upon layer. Afterward the bodies could be brushed so that they looked soft and downy. The eyes were darkened and varnished and the legs and antennae were varnished too, to hold them in shape. Then the wings were drawn and cut out with a fine sharp blade. The best and easiest part was the painting with fine sable paintbrushes. Lemon yellow, lapis blue, brown and black, alizarin crimson to make a dusty ruby.

Clarry always made her butterflies in the sitting room, on a little table in the window, the lightest place in the house. Since the day she had given away the piano, she had never been left alone in that room. Her father could not seem to help hovering distrustfully in the background.

"He thinks you might do it again!" Peter had said once, and Clarry had looked at the clock, whose marble was so pink and fleshy that when she was very little she had supposed it to be meat, and agreed that she possibly might.

Now, as well as her father, Peter was hovering too.

"Tell me when you've finished and I'll tell you where you've gone wrong," he said on the first day.

"Dolls' house games again," complained her father on the second day, which was utterly unfair, since Clarry had never owned a dolls' house, nor even a doll.

"Very clever," said Miss Vane, when the third day arrived. "But you could use prettier shades, pink, or peach or mauve . . . Although even then, I really don't care for the legs!"

"Real butterflies have legs," said Clarry. "I don't think there are pink and peach and mauve ones, though."

"You are quite wrong," said Miss Vane. "I have a vase, Clarry, painted with butterflies in exactly those colors! It was given to me long ago by a great friend and for that reason I keep it on my dressing table between the photo frames. Pink, peach, and mauve. I don't think that yellow you are using looks natural at all."

"There are yellow butterflies just like this one, Miss Vane," said Clarry. "They're quite common in France. Sometimes, when the winds from the south are very strong they get caught in the gale and blown right across the sea. Even as far as Cornwall."

"Clarry, my dear!" exclaimed Miss Vane, sounding suddenly very startled indeed.

"Swallowtails! It's quite true!"

"Clarry!" said Miss Vane, quite urgently and alarmed.

"I read it in a book."

"Clarry, there's a telegram boy outside!"

"A telegram boy? Oh!"

Telegrams in those days of war could be very frightening indeed.

"He's looking toward the house! I think I had better go and speak to him."

Where would a telegram concerning Rupe be sent? Surely not to the grandparents who had become so sad and frail. To this house? To her father?

"Stay here, my dear!" ordered Miss Vane. "I will be very quick."

"No!" cried Clarry, jumping to her feet and overtaking Miss Vane. "NO! Let me!"

But when Clarry held the telegram in her hand she could hardly open it. She shook so hard it was as if some invisible icy force was racketing through her bones.

The most terrible words were: *Missing, presumed dead*.

★　★　★

Although Miss Vane talked too much, and understood too little, and smirked at music and smelled of cats, Clarry never forgot her kindness that day. When the telegram was read Miss Vane guided her to a chair, and wrapped her in a blanket, and gently took it from her hand and laid it on the table beside the half painted butterfly. Her voice sounded cracked and quavering and old, but it did not stop her saying, "There may be hope, there may still be hope," while tears washed wet gray streaks down her powdery cheeks.

Later she brought Clarry a sloppy cup of tea in a clattering saucer. "Where is Peter?" she asked.

"He had to go to Oxford. He's staying the night."

"Your father, Clarry dear? He'll be back quite soon."

He was, but he was useless. He rubbed his neck and stared out of the window and later disappeared.

"Clarry, I must pop home to my cats," said Miss Vane that evening. "I will return very soon and then we will think what to do. All hope is not lost, dear. Many wonderful and astonishing things happen when we least expect them . . ."

When Clarry was alone at last those words echoed in her mind, wonderful and astonishing, wonderful and astonishing. A steady rhythm, like a heartbeat. And despite the fact that she guessed that no part of Miss Vane's experience of life had ever been anywhere near wonderful and astonishing, the words beat on and they kept her from despair and by the time Miss Vane returned she knew what to do.

"Clarry!" said Miss Vane, when she heard.

"You said," Clarry reminded her, "all hope wasn't lost, and perhaps it isn't. And that many wonderful and astonishing things happen and I think sometimes they do, but not in this house."

"No, not in this house," agreed Miss Vane slowly.

"But somewhere else they might," said Clarry, all her old bravery now shining from her eyes. "There are hospitals, in France and in England. There are some in Southampton. That's where I'll begin."

Miss Vane's eyes went to the telegram, still in Clarry's hand.

"Presumed!" said Clarry. "It means they don't know. If I was writing it, I'd put 'Missing, presumed alive!'"

"You would be quite right!" said a suddenly new and bold Miss Vane.

"Peter had a train timetable in his room. I've been looking up trains. There's one in an hour. You needn't worry, Miss Vane. I'll be quite safe."

"I shall not worry and I know you will be safe," said Miss Vane briskly. "Because I intend to come with you, Clarry dear. You may possibly have to go to France, and you do not speak French. Also I can take care of the luggage and deal with the porters. Please do not argue with me."

Clarry did not argue with her. She hugged her instead.

"Many wonderful and astonishing things," she said, smiling through tears, and Miss Vane nodded and hugged her back and said, "Yes. Many wonderful and astonishing things."

Clarry's father was still absent, and the house was still silent, but Clarry and Miss Vane packed unpractical bags and counted their money. Then Clarry picked up the telegram from the table and Miss Vane put down in its place her house key and a list of very detailed cat care instructions.

And so they fled.

Chapter Thirteen

In the time between Christmas and Easter, Binny's life became very busy. There was Max, who needed two good walks a day, besides brushing and feeding. There was Gareth, who demanded daily updates on how they were getting on. There was homework, which had to be done with no excuses, or else Max would get the blame. Also there was Clare, who announced very casually to Binny and Ella one morning at school, "They will start after-school classes in Mandarin Chinese if twelve or more people sign up."

"That's not going to happen, then, is it?" asked Ella (who had turned out to be noisy and funny and very good at drama as well as perpetually hungry).

"Why are you telling us?" demanded Binny (who had turned out to be one of Ella's friends).

"We need two more. It's Wednesdays."

"Ha!" said Ella. "No chance! Not unless you'll come to drama on Tuesdays. Then we can all be in the summer production. *Titanic*. The musical. Perfect for Binny, since she never learned to swim."

Binny said she could not possibly learn Mandarin Chinese or be in *Titanic* the musical because she had Max to walk and homework to endure.

Ella said she had three dogs to walk and a paper round, and Clare said the homework problem could be easily solved if they all joined Homework Club on Mondays and Fridays and got the worst of it out of the way there. Binny pointed out that this only left Thursday with nothing to do, and Ella and Clare looked at her as if she was mad and Ella said, "Don't be silly. It's Photography Group after school on Thursdays. You can't miss that!"

"Every term you get a chance to go on an all-day trip in the minibus," explained Clare.

"And you get let off PE!" added Ella.

"Forever?" asked Binny.

"Just that day," said Ella, "but every little bit helps!"

With all these new things to do, it was amazing how quickly the days and weeks rushed by that term. There came a weekend when Binny found Clare and Mrs. Tremayne in the middle of cleaning the vacation house, ready for summer visitors.

"But it is clean," protested Binny, looking in surprise at the assembled buckets and bleach. "It's very clean! Mum and me and Clem cleaned it, every single bit! Inside the cupboards and under the beds and everywhere! "

"It's stood empty since then, though," said Mrs. Tremayne, and continued emptying shining plates from immaculate cupboards and loading them into the dishwasher to be done on Extra Hot.

"Dust settles. You two go round all the switches please, and check the lightbulbs still come on. Don't forget the bedside lamps and I'll have all the sofa covers off while you're at it."

"Phew!" said Binny rudely.

"Then there's the winter curtains," said Mrs. Tremayne, taking no notice. "They're to go up in the attic, now we've found the key, and I've got the light ones here. Both sets to be washed."

The attic caused fresh outpourings of instructions and bleach. "I'd have the whole lot thrown out," said Mrs. Tremayne, recklessly vacuuming spiders. "But Mark says no, he'll sell it. He'll never find time, though, and even if he did, whoever is going to buy? Those great heavy tennis rackets with all the strings gone, nobody would ever want them! Nor those damp old books, and boxes of rubbish! Whatever have you got there, Binny?"

It was the remains of a hundred-year-old frog skeleton, yellowy wisps of bone on brown mottled card.

"That is *not* hygenic!" said Mrs. Tremayne, whisking it into a trash bag, "and I'll have that case of butterflies too, what's left of them, they're all mildew. Whatever were people thinking of? And they talk about the good old days! What are all those stones?"

"Fossils," said Clare. "Boring."

"We had fossils at school," said Mrs. Tremayne. "Would your school want them? Would that Gareth?"

Gareth had baffled the Tremaynes when Binny had brought him to visit. He had paced the old railway line, inspecting the mud, photographed the shed door, and then offered to sandpaper and paint it.

"It's not the time of year for outdoor painting," the polite Tremaynes had replied. "And you in your good clothes anyway."

Binny had privately admitted that he was a bit weird, but all right when you got used to him, the same as Clem's flute, and James. Now she said, "Gareth would love the fossils," and took the box, with its stones and yellowy labels, all jumbled together.

Peter's fossils, Clarry's labels, Rupe's tennis rackets and a yellowing photograph of him in soldier's uniform. Binny, who loved languages, translated the inscription. "*Good-bye, my friends! See you soon!* But did he see them soon, she wondered, and she asked, "What happened to them? Clarry and Peter and Rupe."

Clarry was easy. Mrs. Tremayne, returning from emptying the vacuumed up spiders into the garden ("*It does them no harm. A change of scene.*"), said, "Clarry. Yes."

"Of course Clare was named for her. Those eyes. Even at ninety. Even at a hundred. She died at a hundred but not before Clare met her. 'The next generation,' she said. 'I wonder what they'll see.' She was pleased about the naming. She never had any children of her own."

"What about Peter? Peter, her brother? What happened to him?"

Peter was not impossible, after they thought to look at the books. Half of them he'd owned, and the other half he'd written. Or so it seemed. There was a thin damp blue one that Binny hugged to her chest:

Origins of Nomenclature in the Animal Kingdom
Clare Penrose (*MA Oxon*) *Peter Penrose* (*PhD Oxon*)

"Please could I borrow it?" Binny begged, and Mrs. Tremayne said, "Goodness, you can keep it."

So the book was rescued from the trash bag as well as the fossils, and so were the painted butterflies, including the Swallowtail. But nowhere in the attic, or in Mrs. Tremayne's memory, was there any news of Rupe.

The tennis rackets went. No use to anyone. The books were repacked to be ignored for another half century or so. The gorse bushes on the moor turned yellow with coconut scented flowers, and Binny and Clare lay amongst them, watching for their mythical beast and swapping the latest news.

"James walked off the pier."

"Fell?"

"Just walked. About a million people jumped in to rescue him but he climbed out himself by the steps."

"Ella's on a diet."

"Titanic?"

"Mmm," said Clare. "There was a lynx, wasn't there?"

"Definitely."

"Do you sometimes wonder?"

"No!" said Binny, indignantly. "We saw it and we rescued it, me and you and . . . Clarry."

Clarry and the painted butterflies, without whom Binny would never have understood Clare and the painted paw prints. Clarry and Peter and Rupe.

"What did happen to Rupe?" demanded Binny sternly.

At first Clare wouldn't think. She said, "Does it matter, really? It was ages ago."

"He was a soldier in the war," persisted Binny. "Me and Clem looked it up after we found that photograph. It was terrible. All mud and dying and bombs like fireworks and poor old horses like in that book they made us read for English. Awful!"

"I quite liked it. There's a film now."

"The *war* was awful," said Binny. "Not the book! Loads of people died. Loads. Why didn't Clarry finish painting the Swallowtail butterfly for Rupe?"

"Because . . . because she didn't need to. He came back, suddenly, so she didn't need to! Or else, because he died. Don't look like that! He might have done. Lots did. You said so yourself."

"I don't want him to have died. You met Clarry. You actually met her! Was she sad?"

"Bin! I was about one and she was about a hundred!"

"So you can't remember?"

"Of *course* I can't remember!"

"I only asked. In case. I can remember nearly everything that happened when I was one. Carpet burns. Flying round the room. Everything."

Clare gave her a look.

"Think of it like a story," said Binny, ignoring it. "We haven't reached the end."

"Because it isn't a story," said Clare. "It's just broken bits of things that happened."

"They're what stories are made of," said Binny. "They join up, and you get a new one. If James hadn't lost his chicken Mark wouldn't have gone out with his gun. If Gareth hadn't noticed the paw print I wouldn't ever have known about the lynx. If Clarry hadn't painted butterflies I would never have understood why you painted paw prints. The lynx wouldn't have been saved. Think! If Clarry hadn't painted butterflies we wouldn't be here now!"

Clare listened to all this.

"This lynx, it's gone," said Binny. "It's traveled out of the story. But Rupe. Did he die in the war, or not?"

"You don't go to church," said Clare.

"No."

"Outside the church is the war memorial. With all the names on it of everyone who died. Everyone from this town. In the first war and the second."

"There were two?"

"Don't you know anything?"

"I don't know *everything*," said Binny. "Come on!"

The wind helped. It came buffeting across the country, straight from the south. It blew them back over the moor and it was behind them on the long road into town.

They crossed the star shaped marketplace and there was the high wall that surrounded the church, with the gate at one end.

And suddenly there was the war memorial, a high granite cross on a great gray plinth. Words were carved on the cross, and lists of names on the plinth. Long columns, all four sides covered.

Binny was shocked. She hadn't expected so many names. Of course Rupe must be there. Why should he have escaped, when so many others had not? She caught sight of an *R* and turned her eyes away and then looked again.

COBLEY R.

Not Rupe, then, good.

Although not good for R. Cobley, whoever he was, thought Binny guiltily, and read further:

COBLEY T.

COBLEY W. A.

All at once Binny couldn't read anymore. She ached for the stricken Cobleys. She didn't want to find PENROSE R.

Clare was not hurrying to search the names either. She was squinting to make out the words carved on the cross.

She read them aloud. " *'To strive, to seek, to find, and not to yield.'* I don't know about not yielding," she said, sounding just like her mother. "I'd probably have yielded. I do it all the time at home. Are you looking for Rupe, or not?"

"I don't know now. It feels like snooping," said Binny uncomfortably, and was relieved when Clare said at once, "That's exactly what it feels like! Like at school when you read the register upside down to see everyone else's marks! Do you want to come inside and see my font where I was christened?" She headed to the church door without waiting for a reply.

Binny did not follow. A movement had caught her eye. Inside the high wall the churchyard was sheltered from the wind. The wall itself was lined with bushes. They had greeny gray leaves and long triangular flower heads hanging down like purple bunting. They were butterfly bushes and the movement Binny had seen was butterflies. Dozens of butterflies. Brown and amber, black and scarlet, peacock patterned, paper white, checkered, splashed, and streaked and silver.

"Clare!" she shrieked.

There before her lucky eyes was a butterfly much larger than the rest. Lemon yellow.

"Clare! Clare!"

"What?" asked Clare, shooting out of the church door. "What is it? Stop shouting! You're not supposed to shout here."

"Look!"

"Oh!" exclaimed Clare, suddenly seeing. "It isn't! It is! It's huge! It's gorgeous!"

"It's one of Clarry's butterflies," said Binny. "It's a Swallowtail."

Sometimes, once or twice every hundred years or so, when necessary (perhaps), when the wind is from the south, yellow butterflies arrive in Cornwall, blown from France like messages.

Time stopped while Binny and Clare watched the Swallowtail cruise between the flowers, pausing for moments, rising again.

"Perfect," whispered Clare, and even as she spoke, it lifted on the air and was gone. Binny sighed. Clare looked over her shoulder at the war memorial.

"He's not there," said Binny, "that was to tell us," and they looked, and he wasn't.

For a while they were quiet, silent with thoughts.

"But where did it come from?" asked Clare at last.

"From the wind. From the sky. From a hundred years ago."

"I'm glad he was all right," said Clare.

They wandered home. Across the old tennis courts

where the echo of balls was like a rhythm in the air, even though the courts had been a car park for nearly forty years. Pausing at the haunted book shop to watch the boy with the limp push back his dark hair, turn a page, drop his head again. The wind, that had blown itself into a gale, had blown itself out again, and dropped to stillness. A kestrel passed overhead with a call like a small bell. They walked more and more slowly, and they talked of the future now, not of the past.

"I've been wondering," said Clare. "Do you think the lynx might meet another lynx?"

For a moment Binny was silenced by this lovely thought, and then she said, "It's sure to do! In all that space, it's got to do! Probably has already!"

"Lynx cubs!"

"Lynx kittens! Gareth will be pleased!"

"Could it really happen? Would it fit into the story?"

"Oh," said Binny. "Easily! That's the best thing about stories. Once you start to live in them, anything can happen."

Turn the page to discover the beloved Casson Family in **Saffy's Angel!**

WHEN SAFFRON WAS EIGHT, AND HAD AT LAST LEARNED TO read, she hunted slowly through the color chart pinned up on the kitchen wall.

It was a painter's color chart, from an artists' materials shop. It showed all the colors a painter could ever need. There were rows and rows of little squares, each a different shade of red or blue or green or golden yellow. Every little square had the name of the color underneath. To the Casson children those names were as familiar as nursery rhymes. Other families had lullabies, but the Cassons had fallen asleep to lists of colors.

Saffron found Indigo almost at once, a smoky dark blue on the bottom row of the chart. Indigo was two years younger than Saffron. His name suited him exactly.

"If there is one thing your mother was good at," Bill Casson, the children's father, would say, "it was choosing names for you children!"

Eve, the children's mother, would always look pleased. She never protested that there might be more than one thing that she was good at, because she never thought there was.

Indigo was a thin, dark-haired little boy with anxious indigo-colored eyes. He had a list in his head of things that did not matter (such as school), and another list of things that did. High on Indigo's list of things that mattered was his pack. That was how he thought of his sisters. His pack.

Saffron was the middle one of the pack.

Saffron had to climb onto a stool to see the color chart properly. The stool had a top of woven string that was coming unwoven, and its legs rocked on the irregular tiles of the kitchen floor.

"I can't find me," she grumbled to Indigo, wobbling on the stool. "I can't find *Saffron* written anywhere."

"What about the rest of us?" asked Indigo, not looking up. "What about the baby?"

Indigo was crouched on the hearth rug, sorting through the coal bucket. Pieces of coal lay all around. Sometimes he found lumps speckled with what he believed to be gold. He looked like a small black devil in the shadowy room with the firelight behind him.

"Come and help me look for Saffron!" pleaded Saffron.

"Find the baby first," said Indigo.

Indigo did not like the baby to be left out of anything that was going on. This was because for a long time after she was born, it had seemed she would be left out of everything, and forever. She had very nearly eluded his pack. She had very nearly died. Now she was safe and easy to find, third row up at the end of the pinks. Rose. Permanent Rose.

Rose was screaming because the health visitor had arrived to look at her. She had turned up unexpectedly, from beyond the black, rainy windows, and picked up Rose with her strong, cold hands, and so Rose was screaming.

"Make Rose shut up!" shouted Saffron from her stool. "I'm trying to read!"

"Saffron reads anything now!" the children's mother told the health visitor proudly.

"Very nice!" the health visitor replied, and Saffron looked pleased for a moment, but then stopped when the health visitor added that both her twins had been fluent readers at four years old and had gone right through their elementary school library by the age of six.

Saffron glanced across to Caddy, the eldest of the Casson children, to see if this could possibly be true. Caddy, aged thirteen, was absorbed in painting the soles of her hamster's feet, but she felt Saffron's unhappiness and gave her a quick, comforting smile. Since Rose's arrival the Casson family had heard an awful lot about the health visitor's multitalented twins. They were in Caddy's class at school. There were a number of rude and true things that Caddy might have said about them, but being Caddy, she kept them to herself. Her smile was enough.

Caddy appeared over and over on the color chart, all along the top row. Cadmium Lemon, Cadmium Deep Yellow, Cadmium Scarlet, and Cadmium Gold.

No Saffron, though.

"There *isn't* a Saffron," said Saffron after another long search. "I've looked, and there isn't! I've read it all, and there *isn't*!"

Nobody seemed to hear at first. Caddy continued painting her hamster's feet. The baby continued screaming. Eve continued explaining to the health visitor (who frightened her very much) that she had not noticed anything at all wrong with Rose until the health visitor pointed it out, and the health visitor continued tut-tutting.

"I can't find Saffron!" complained Saffron crossly.

Indigo said, "Saffron's yellow."

"I *know* Saffron's yellow!"

"Well then, look under the yellows," Indigo said, and tipped the whole of the coal bucket upside down on the hearth, enveloping his end of the room in a cloud of coal dust.

This made the health visitor start coughing as well as tutting.

"I don't know how you keep your patience!" she said to Eve. Her voice showed that she thought it would be much better if Eve did not. She had dropped in to weigh Rose, as she often did, and had noticed at once that the baby had gone a very strange color. A sort of brownish mustard. She seemed to think it was a terrible thing that Rose should have gone mustard without anybody noticing. She began undressing her.

"I've looked under *all* the yellows," said Saffron loudly and belligerently, "and I've looked under *all* the oranges too, and there *isn't* a Saffron!"

Rose wailed even louder because she didn't want to be undressed. Her mother said, "Oh, darling! Darling!" Indigo began hammering at likely-looking lumps of coal with the handle end of the poker. Caddy let the hamster walk across the table, and it made a delicate and beautiful pattern of rainbow-colored footprints all over the health visitor's notes.

"*Why* isn't there a Saffron?" demanded Saffron. "There's all the others. What about me?"

Then the health visitor said the thing that changed Saffron's life. She looked up from picking something out of Rose's clenched fist and said to the children's mother, "Doesn't Saffron know?"

The words fell into a moment of silence. Rose held her breath between roars. Caddy's head jerked up and her eyes were startled. Indigo stopped hammering. Eve went scarlet and looked very confused and began an unhappy mumble. A not-yet, not-now sort of mumble.

"Know what?" asked Saffron, looking from the health visitor to her mother.

"Nothing, dear," said the health visitor in a bright, careless voice, and Saffron, who was frightened without knowing why, allowed herself to believe this was true.

"Nothing, nothing!" repeated the health visitor, half singing the words, and then in a completely different voice, "Good heavens! What on earth is this?"

Rose's fist had come undone, revealing that she held a tube of paint (Yellow Ochre), obviously very much sucked.

"Paint!" said the health visitor, absolutely horrified. "*Paint!* PAINT! She's had a tube of paint! This household . . . I don't know! *She's been sucking a tube of paint!*"

"What color?" asked Indigo immediately.

"Yellow Ochre," Caddy told him. "I gave it to her. I didn't think she'd suck it. Anyway, I'm only using nontoxic colors."

"Caddy!" said her mother, laughing. "No wonder she's gone such a funny color!"

"I'm ringing the hospital!" said the health visitor in a voice of controlled calm. "Wrap her up in something warm! Don't give her anything to drink! We'll go straight to Emergency. . . ."

Then for a while Saffron forgot her worries while they all tried to convince the health visitor that none of Caddy's colors were in the least poisonous, and that Rose, except for needing washing, was quite all right.

"But *why* did you give it to her?" the health visitor asked Caddy.

"To make her let go of the Chinese White," said Caddy.

"Chinese White's sweet," explained Saffron, and then there was another fuss. While it was going on, Indigo got bored and went back to his gold hunting, bashing a lump of coal so hard that pieces flew everywhere, and the baby got a chunk to suck, and the hamster jumped in fright into the health visitor's bag, and the health visitor said, "Thank goodness my twins . . . ! If that hamster has made a mess . . . I suppose this is what they call artistic. . . ."

"Yes," said Eve eagerly. "They are all very—"

"You need the patience of a saint in my job!" said the health visitor as she left.

After she had gone, the children's mother hunted through the kitchen cupboards looking for something for supper. While she was doing it, she cried a bit because it was so hard being an artist with four children to look after, especially in wet weather, when rain blew under the kitchen door and down all the chimneys and into the hood of the car so that it would not start and she could not get to the supermarket. She thought wistfully of the shed at the end of the garden, her favorite place in the world.

Only Rose noticed she was crying. Rose watched her with unsurprised blue eyes, enjoying the sniffs.

The kitchen cupboard was full of nonfood sorts of food. Lentils and cereal and packaged sauces and jam. Eve had almost given up hope when she unearthed a large and completely unexpected can of baked beans, the sort with sausages in it, a small miracle.

"Daddy must have bought them!" she exclaimed, as happy as she had been miserable a moment before.

The beans changed everything. Saffron took over the toaster. Caddy put the hamster into its cage and cleared the table. Indigo picked up his lumps of coal. Permanent Rose sucked a crust of bread and smiled at everyone and waited patiently until someone should think of scrambling her an egg. Eve stirred the beans and sausages and was grateful to the children's father. He was a real artist, not a garden-shed one like herself. He was such a very real artist that he could work only in London. He rented a small studio at enormous expense and came home only on weekends. Real artists, he often explained to Caddy and Saffron and Indigo, cannot work with three children under their feet and a baby that wakes up several times every night.

"Clever, clever Daddy, buying beans!" said Eve.

"Rose could have an egg," suggested Caddy, reading Rose's mind.

"I wonder if Dad bought anything else," said Indigo, and he and Saffron at once began searching the kitchen cupboards themselves, hoping for more surprises. A lump of coal turned up, with a glitter of gold on it, and a bag of squashed pink and white marshmallows, which they floated on hot chocolate and shared with Rose from the end of a spoon. It was a very happy evening and bedtime before Saffron asked again, "Why isn't my name on the color chart? Why isn't there a Saffron?"

"Saffron is a lovely color," said her mother evasively.

"But it's not on the chart."

"Well . . ."

"The others are."

"Yes."

"But not me."

"I thought of calling you Siena. Or Scarlet."

"Why didn't you?"

There was a long, long pause.

"It wasn't me who chose your name."

"Dad?"

"No. Not Daddy. My sister."

"Your sister who died?"

"Yes. Go to sleep, Saffy. Rose is crying. I've got to go."

"Siena," whispered Saffy.

Saffy had a dream that came over and over. In the dream was a white paved place with walls. A sunny place, quiet and enclosed. There were little dark, pointed trees and there was the sound of water. The blue sky was too bright to look at. In the dream something was lost. In the dream Saffy cried. In the dream was the word, *Siena*.

Caddy's bed was close enough to touch. Saffy could tell by the feel of the darkness that Caddy was awake. She said, "Caddy, how long ago can you remember?"

"Oh," said Caddy, "ages. I can remember when I could only lie flat. On my back. I can remember how pleased I was when I learned to roll over."

"You can't!"

"I can. And I remember learning to crawl. It hurt my knees."

"No one can remember that far back!"

"Well, I can. I remember it quite clearly. The burny feeling it gave my knees."

"Do you remember a white stone garden?"

"What white stone garden?"

"Siena."

"No," said Caddy. "That was you, not me."

The next morning Indigo gave Saffron his gold-speckled lump of coal, and Cadmium added an extra color square to the top row of the paint chart, Saffron Yellow. In London, Bill Casson shut up his small (and very expensive) studio midweek and caught the first train home.

None of these things meant anything at all to Saffron. All she could think of was the terrible news that she had forced from Eve the night before. Bit by bit, while Rose slept and Indigo argued and Caddy watched and was silent, Saffron had dragged it out.

That was how she discovered that Eve was not her mother. Nor was a real (and nearly successful) artist in London her father. Worst of all, Caddy and Indigo and Rose were not her brother and sisters.

"You're not my family," said Saffron.

"We are!" cried Eve. "Of course we are! We adopted you! We wanted you! Your mother was my sister! Caddy and Indigo and Rose are your cousins!"

"That doesn't count," said Saffron.

"I'm not doing this right," said Eve, weeping. "There are books on how to do it right. I have read them. You were only three. You looked just like Caddy. You called me Mummy.

You were so happy. Almost as soon as you arrived, you were happy!"

"Why was it a secret?"

"It wasn't a secret!" protested Eve, trying to hug Saffron (who ducked). "I was waiting for the right time to tell you, that's all. And the longer I left it, the harder it was. I should have done it right at the start!"

"Caddy knew! And didn't tell me!"

"I forgot," said Caddy.

"Forgot!"

"Nearly always."

"No wonder I'm not on the color chart," said Saffron.

Everything seemed to change for Saffron after the

day she deciphered the color chart and discovered that her name was not there and found out why this was. She never felt the same again. She felt lost.

"But everything is just the same," said Bill, trying to help.

"Nothing has changed, Saffy darling. We love you just as much as we ever did. You are just as much ours as you always were."

"No, I'm not," said Saffy.

Eve produced photographs of Saffy's mother, but they were very confusing. Saffron's mother had been Eve's twin sister. They were so alike that even Eve had to puzzle over some of the pictures before she could say who was who.

"What about my father?" Saffron asked.

This was a difficult question. Saffron's mother had never told Eve anything about Saffron's father.

"Your mummy never talked about him," she said at last.

"Not even to you?"

"Well," said Eve, sighing as she remembered. "She was in Italy and I was in England. So it was difficult. I was always going to go and visit her, and I never quite did. I wish I had."